Victor whispered softly to her until they ended up together on their sides f⸻**
each other. She** ⸻
slowly floated ba⸻

"I'm sorry I walked ou⸻
whispered.

"I know."

His breath brushed against her mouth. She dug her fingers into his bared chest, giving herself over to the wet movement of her mouth against his. Then he pulled abruptly away from her.

"Someone is coming."

She didn't question how he knew, just scrambled to her feet and yanked down her dress. By the time she had herself together, he was already zipped up, shirt buttoned and black blazer back on. But his eyes were still tender in the silver glow of the moon. She wanted to kiss him again. Mella deliberately stepped away from him when she heard the approaching footsteps for herself.

"I should go." She clasped her purse tightly against her thighs, turning her back to the path so she wouldn't see who was coming. Resentment at the intruders lay heavy and bitter at the back of her throat.

Dear Reader,

Have you ever had such tragedy in your life that the only thing you can do is face the world with a determined smile? That's what Mella does on a daily basis… faking happy until she feels it. But running into the difficult and handsome Victor Raphael shakes her very foundation, including her smile. And there's more than the sizzling attraction between them. Mella senses that underneath Victor's growling surface is someone with demons as savage as her own. Despite the pain of the past, will these two beasts collide and manage to make beautiful music together?

Come with me, and follow their journey.

Lindsay Evans

Untamed
LOVE

Lindsay Evans

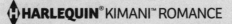
HARLEQUIN® KIMANI™ ROMANCE

Recycling programs
for this product may
not exist in your area.

ISBN-13: 978-0-373-86439-3

Untamed Love

For questions and comments about the quality of this book please contact us at CustomerService@Harlequin.com.

Printed in U.S.A.

Lindsay Evans was born in Jamaica and currently lives and writes in Atlanta, Georgia, where she's constantly on the hunt for inspiration, club in hand. She loves good food and romance and would happily travel to the ends of the earth for both. Find out more at lindsayevanswrites.com.

Books by Lindsay Evans

Harlequin Kimani Romance

Pleasure Under the Sun
Sultry Pleasure
Snowy Mountain Nights
Affair of Pleasure
Untamed Love

To my readers, old and new.
Thank you for sharing your time with me.

Acknowledgments

This writing journey of mine wouldn't be possible
without Sheree L. Greer, Angela Gabriel,
Cherie Evans Lyon and Dorothy Lindsay.
As my beta reader, Sheree has read more romance novels
than she'd ever even thought possible, and Angela
has suffered with me through many plotting sessions
over dinner and ice cream. Cherie Evans Lyon and
Dorothy Lindsay have simply *always* been there.

Kimberly Kaye Terry, as ever, thank you.

Chapter 1

"If you weren't my friend, I'd be burying your body out back right now." Victor Raphael carefully put a hand on the cloth-covered table in front of him, the other hand balanced on his thigh as he listened to the auctioneer call out to the eager bidders.

"Three thousand, five hundred dollars!" the tuxedoed man shouted, his teeth a blinding white in his tanned face. "Do I hear four thousand?"

His best friend, Kingsley Diallo, didn't look worried. "Auctioning yourself off for charity will make you feel good," he said with a vague smile, looking around the large ballroom of one of their acquaintance's latest mansion renovation projects gone wrong. Naked cherubs everywhere. "And it'll make you look like less of an ass."

Kingsley, perpetually Miami casual in a lavender V-neck shirt and celebrity-endorsed jeans, eventually settled back in his chair across from Victor, apparently satisfied that he had checked out the entire room and seen what there was to see. Victor, however, was quietly furious. Kingsley had put the services of his company up for bid without him knowing. Victor was a landscape architect, not some bored socialite's puppet. He opened his mouth to say as much, but the auctioneer announced Raphael Design Group, effectively shutting him up. Victor snapped his eyes back to the small raised stage in the center of the room.

They were doing things the old-fashioned way, raising paddles to signal their interest in the bids. Despite the open ballroom, brightly lit by the afternoon sun, the French doors were open to let in the crisp February breeze. Or at least as crisp as February ever got in Miami. Every event like this Victor had ever seen on TV took place in shadowed rooms or unironically old European auction houses with the look of old blood money staining the silk-papered walls. But this was Miami. Why wouldn't things be different? He'd half expected a stripper parading around in a white thong and moaning the name of each item up for bid. But maybe that spoke to his lack of class.

Despite the fact that it was his services on the line, Victor tuned out the proceedings. It didn't matter who won. Kingsley had decided that Victor should get out of his comfort zone and had damn near pushed him out of it, so here he was, obligated to perform. For free.

His fingers flexed on top of his thighs, the muscles

tense and strained. Just like the rest of him. Polite applause rippled through the room. Someone had won the auction. His fingers tightened even more.

"Nice one." Kingsley reached over the small table to clap him on the shoulder.

Would it really be that bad to shovel dirt over his best friend's face and leave him for dead? Maybe someone would find his traitorous body after an hour or two.

Ice cubes rattled in a glass, and he looked down to see a tumbler of ginger beer in front of him, along with a slice of German chocolate cake. He gave Kingsley a grim look but picked up the glass. The liquid was cool and stroked his tongue and throat with its effervescence as it went down.

"One day, I will kill you," he said.

"Not today, my friend." Kingsley drank from his own glass: whiskey neat. "Today, you'll thank me."

"I doubt that."

Kingsley laughed as if he knew a secret. He dug into his own slice of chocolate cake, a dessert that was a favorite for them both. His friend was relying on bribery to soothe his temper. The cake was good, he'd grant Kingsley that.

The auction was the last event of the fund-raiser, an afternoon garden party to raise money to help local low-income kids pay for college. Victor breathed a sigh of relief that it was almost over. Soon he would get in his car and drive back to his house in the upper east side of the city, maybe even pick something up from Whole Foods to cook for dinner.

"All right!" Kingsley's fork rattled against the now-empty dessert plate. "Let's go meet the winner." He picked up his whiskey.

"No. I'm done with this." Being social wasn't Victor's forte.

His sister had even called him a standoffish hermit, which he'd told her was a bit redundant. He'd already donated money to the scholarship fund and even wished the high schoolers good luck, although he winced in sympathy, for them, being paraded in front of these rich idiots just so they could feel sorry for the kids and see that their money wasn't going to waste. Or something equally stupid.

"Come on, man. You have to see who won." Kingsley nudged him to his feet. "Not to mention you need to make arrangements to start the work."

"That's what phones are for." But he allowed himself to be led across the room toward the table where the winning bidders gathered with the auctioneer and his half dozen or so assistants.

"The winning number is 191," Kingsley hissed as they stepped into the sea of designer casual wear and perfumes.

Before Victor left his house to come to the auction, the day hadn't been especially good. He was thinking about his sister Violet as he always did on her birthday, his already dour mood plummeting with the thought that she would have been thirty this year.

Kingsley apparently knew him too well and called to drag him out of the house and into the light of social interaction. Too bad he had no idea before he left the house of the knife Kingsley was gleefully waiting to plunge into his back. The bastard.

At a far table, he spotted a black-and-white paddle with the number Kingsley told him. *Better get this over with sooner rather than later*, he thought. He pushed through the crowd toward the older man who held the paddle upside down in the crook of his crossed arms.

Kingsley grabbed him. "Where are you going?"

He jerked his head toward the man holding the number of the winning bid.

But Kingsley shook his head. "Wrong number." He squeezed Victor's arm and pointed toward another paddle, this one held in a slender feminine hand: 191. As he watched, the woman slowly began to fan her face with the paddle. Victor swallowed.

The sight of her punched the breath from his lungs. She was damn stunning. Hair in tight and gorgeous coils around her face, skin the warm brown of the inside of a seashell. The perfect handful everywhere. And so very unlike any woman he'd ever seen that he nearly stumbled on his way to her.

It was only Kingsley's amused presence at his side that kept Victor from tripping over his own feet. Even from across the room, there was something about the way she made him feel that beat a hard and familiar drum deep inside him. It was like fear and exhilaration all at once.

She fanned her face, and the small breeze from the auction paddle stirred the cottony hair resting around her cheeks. That hair was big, springy and wild, framing narrow and laughing eyes. One of the two women around her laughed, too, then leaned in to slap play-fully at her shoulder. Her friends, Victor assumed. Two women who were pretty enough in their tight outfits, with their laughing faces and sophisticated clothes.

Next to them, the woman looked like their little sister, almost innocent in her white blazer, pale floral slacks that tapered down to her narrow calves and high-heeled pink shoes. A big necklace in the shape of a sunflower rested at her throat. She was springtime personified. From the first glance, there was nothing sensual about her, only joy in the way she stood, a radiant presence in the crowd. Then she tipped her head back with the paddle moving languorously through the air, revealing more of her slender neck, the line of her jaw. And desire bit him low in his belly.

"You all right, man?"

Kingsley's question should have worried Victor. He was showing too much emotion. He shouldn't care. He should tighten up and exchange information with the winner of the bid and then leave. But all he could do was feel and realize that no, he was not all right. Far from it.

"This place is such a madhouse." Mella used her auction paddle to fan her face. "And it's hot." She grinned. This was the kind of scene she loved. The restrained wildness of the crowd, the heated wave of everyone's intentions as they surged toward something they wanted. Even if it was just bidding for a vacuum-cleaning service. She fanned a little faster, wondering what drove the organizers to open the doors of the massive ballroom instead of turning on the AC. This was Miami, not freakin' Minneapolis.

"This so-called party is about as much fun as watching paint dry in the cold, Mella." Corinne looked the epitome of boredom in her Gucci shades that she refused to take off indoors. It probably had something to do with her red eyes and the late night she'd had the day before.

"Relax, Corinne." Mella glanced over at her friend, reining in her smile. "You'll get the chance to throw yourself at eligible single men in just a few minutes. I need to get the information about the landscape guy, then we can go." She'd already paid for her winning bid and was only waiting to collect her prize.

"Yeah. Relax, Corinne." Liz, Mella's best friend and Corinne's old college roommate, sucked in her stomach and posed in her barely decent dress. Her high heels put her already tall frame nearly half a head over most women in the room, including Mella, who could only claim five feet. "You need to smell the roses. Or in this case, the testosterone. Maybe the guy Mella bid on is some hot and hung lumberjack type wearing jeans tight enough for me to tell his religion."

Mella snorted with laughter. "You're thinking about a gardener, not a landscape architect."

"Same thing," Liz muttered.

Mella heard Corinne take in a quick breath and whisper under her breath, "No, it's not." Corinne took off her dark glasses and stared.

Mella turned to see what her friend was gawking at. Only through an act of will did she keep the paddle in her hand moving, fluttering the air around her face that suddenly felt several degrees too hot. Two men were walking purposefully toward them. She bit the inside of her lip to keep her mouth from dropping open just like Corinne's. Of the two men stalking their way, she only really noticed one.

He was dressed all in black, an utter contrast to everyone else at the fund-raiser who'd put on their spring colors and lightweight jackets. Black upon black upon black. Leather ankle boots with an understated sheen, Italian-cut slacks that fit a lean shape and a dress shirt rolled up to show muscled and lightly veined forearms dusted with hair. His watch, a gleaming stainless steel, was the only touch of light on him.

"Damn, he's fine!" Corinne breathed somewhere near Mella.

"Yes, girl…" Mella could only agree while she lost her breath to the man in black.

There was nothing pretty or soft about him. Watching him walk through the crowd and make his way toward where she and her friends stood was like watching a jaguar stalk through a room of gazelles, the silken glide of his every step a promise of power and strength. Mella's back straightened, but she felt her legs quiver from the impending confrontation. She kept the smile on her face.

"They both are," Liz said with an amazed laugh. "After seeing absolutely nobody halfway decent in here for the past two hours, and now these two fine gods walk in from nowhere…somebody up there was listening to my prayers."

From the corner of her eye, Mella noticed Corinne preen even more, smoothing a hand down her taut thighs and shifting toward the men in profile so they could admire the high curve of her butt in the clinging white jumpsuit. "Maybe we can get one for you at the next spot, Mella." She said the last nearly under her breath since the men had come steadily closer and were only a few feet from them.

Mella continued to fan her face, wishing desperately for the heat in her cheeks to subside. She never reacted like this to men. Never.

"My name is Victor Raphael." The one in black held out his hand for Mella to shake. "I believe you've won me for the next few months." Just as his look promised, his voice was a lulling purr, calm and steady. A man used to giving orders and having them obeyed. "I'm with Raphael Design Group," he said after a short pause.

Damn, he's tall. She stared up and up at him. Then looked down at his hand, not quite ready to touch him yet. It felt like a big step for her to take his hand and feel his skin against hers, to know some of the strength in him. She looked down at the large hand, at least larger than her own, and opened her mouth to speak. But Corinne slid close and grasped Victor Raphael's hand instead.

"I'm Corinne," she said. "I haven't won you, but you can win me."

Her friend's foolishness snapped Mella out of her daze. "Michaela Davis." She introduced herself with a nod and smile, then turned to his friend who she'd barely noticed. "And you are?"

"Kingsley Diallo." His friend shook her hand with a wide smile. "I wasn't won and didn't win anything. I'm just here for the food." Laugh lines bracketed his expressive mouth.

Mella liked him immediately. "Wasn't the lobster mac and cheese phenomenal?"

Kingsley laughed, an infectious sound that had her instantly laughing with him. "It was," he said. "Although I have had much better from a friend's kitchen."

"Let's get back to the business of this auction before we discuss the menu." Victor said the last word like a curse. Didn't he like food?

Well, two could play at that all-business game. Mella held out her hand. "Your card?"

For a moment, he stared hard at her, at her hand. Then reached for his wallet and took out a business card. She was surprised that it wasn't black, too. Instead it was a crisp green with black writing, everything she needed to contact him, including a QR code printed on the back.

"Call me when you're ready," he said.

"I'm ready now," Liz muttered behind Mella.

Mella ignored her friend and gave Victor a card of her own, taking care that their fingers didn't touch. Would their hands spark with static electricity, or would it be like touching any other man? She wasn't quite ready to find out.

Normally, she would have grasped him in one of her typically friendly handshakes, a handshake that would morph into a hug at their next meeting, but she had a feeling he wasn't like every other man she'd dealt with before. She tucked his card away into her purse and clenched her teeth into a determined smile.

"Perfect." She gripped her purse and tapped it against the front of her thighs, almost succeeding in ignoring Victor and the weakening effect he had on her. Her heart was practically fighting to leap out of her chest. "It was good to meet you both, but now we have to head out. Have a great afternoon."

"But wait…they just got here." Corinne sounded as if she was working up to a pout. She and Liz had been chatting up Kingsley while Mella and Victor "got down to business."

Liz put a hand on Kingsley's forearm. "We were heading to Fever on South Beach. They're having a huge day party. You should come with." Did she just bat her eyes?

Corinne, who could read most men as easily as her daily horoscope, turned her attention to Kingsley instead of trying to worm her way beneath Victor's aloof and prickly exterior. He was obviously not into playing anyone's game. Mella couldn't help but chuckle at the Cheshire Cat grin that took over Kingsley's face as the two women latched on to him on either side.

"You ladies could tempt a monk to sin," he said, although he was obviously *not* a monk.

Why couldn't Mella have been attracted to him? He looked fun, as if he was open to wherever the night might take him and would simply leave it all behind the next morning, no strings attached. Instead she was aware of every breath that left Victor Raphael's body, of the firm heat of him only a few feet away, aware of just how much she wanted to twine her arms around his waist and lead him into breathless sin. But she didn't need to know his sun sign to realize he wasn't that kind of man. She kept her smile easy and noncommittal.

"You can go ahead, Kingsley." Victor tipped his head toward the open door through which most of the party's attendees had already gone. "You've had a long week at the office and need some time to unwind. You're not going to get that from me today. I can get a cab back home."

The two men exchanged a private look. Then Kingsley glanced down at the women, obviously tempted to stay with them. But he shook his head, about to speak.

Mella jumped in. "There's no need to ruin anybody's night, Kingsley. I can take Victor home, and you go with Corinne and Liz. He and I can talk business while you three have fun. I need to head home early, anyway." For what exactly, she didn't know. But if playing chauffeur meant she could spend a few minutes longer in Victor's company, then it would be a pleasure.

Kingsley turned to his friend with a raised brow. "Only if Victor is okay with that plan," he said.

Mella couldn't look at Victor. With one stroke of his commanding gaze, she felt all her good sense begin to desert her. God! This was humiliating. But she couldn't think of any place else she'd rather be. Victor made a low noise, which finally urged her to look at him. Although his face was blank, it was obvious he didn't want to go to Fever.

"No," he said. "I'd need more than an *almost* handshake for you to take me home."

Did he just make a joke? Mella blinked at Victor.

"I'll come with you to the day party," he said. "As Kingsley is quick to say, I need to get out of the house, anyway."

Oh.

"Okay." Mella rolled her eyes as her friends highfived each other. She hoped Victor Raphael knew what he was getting himself into.

They left the party in two separate cars, with Victor and Kingsley agreeing to meet them at Fever. The men already knew where the place was, or at least Kingsley did.

"I don't know what you guys were thinking inviting them to the party. Victor didn't look like he was in the mood." Mella was a big fan of doing what she wanted instead of what other people expected. Life just tended to be happier that way.

From the small backseat of Mella's green Fiat convertible, Corinne giggled. "We would have been happy just hanging with Kingsley. He seemed fun, at least."

Mella glared at her in the rearview mirror, annoyed that she would think of leaving Victor behind, even if that meant Mella would get the chance to take him home. She didn't dwell too long on how that sounded in her head. "But what would Kingsley look like, leaving his friend for some random chicks he just met?"

"Spontaneous, Mella. He'd look spontaneous."

Mella shook her head. She was all for spontaneous, but she was about loyalty, too. And she liked that, though it was a small thing, Kingsley had stuck by his friend even when it seemed he could have gotten lucky, twice, on his own. Mella knew her friends weren't above the occasional threesome. They may have been on the marriage hunt, but she knew they saw nothing wrong with having a little fun along the way.

"You all are dead wrong," she muttered.

At Fever, the music was loud and bass-heavy, women and men in tight designer clothes, the liquor flowing freely on the wide rooftop. The three women headed for the bar for their usual drinks before looking for Victor and Kingsley. When they found them, Kingsley was dancing in the middle of the crowded floor with a woman Mella was fairly certain he'd never met before.

Victor, though, was nowhere to be seen. Her friends flocked to Kingsley, ready to fend off the Jenny-come-lately who was hanging on to his hips for dear life as they grooved to the hip-hop pounding from the speakers.

She saw some people she already knew and joined them, leaving her husband-hunting friends to make their move on Kingsley. The afternoon was fun and the music and energy all that Mella hoped for. She drank her cocktails, shared gossip with old friends and danced until the sweat ran down her back and she had to take off her blazer and leave it hanging on the back of a chair.

It wasn't long before she finished her second drink and wanted another one, but the main bar had a line from hell. She excused herself from her friends and made her way to the other side of Fever and downstairs to the hidden bar very few people knew about. Mella gripped the chrome handrails and nearly stumbled down the stairs in her high heels, her thighs trembling faintly from dancing for nearly two hours straight in her stilettos.

The lower level of Fever was smaller than the rooftop space, surrounded by floor-to-ceiling windows letting in the bright Miami sunlight. But the bar, hanging as it was beneath dark beams and sheltered from much of the brightness, was partially in shadows.

Barely a half dozen people sat at the stools surrounding the bar. The patrons that sat on the stools were spread out, little islands to themselves. One man and woman were practically sitting in each other's laps, an impressive feat considering the small size of the bar stools, a trio of businessmen and a lone man dressed in black who sat with his back to the room. Mella went up to the bar, fitting herself between the businessmen and the man in black. She signaled the bartender, who had been talking amicably with the lone man.

The bartender turned. "Hey, Mella." His bright smile lit up his entire face.

"Hey yourself, Greg. How have you been?" She gave him her order, a Blood and Sand, and propped her hip against one of the bar stools.

"I'm doing great now that you're at my bar." He amped up his smile.

"You say the loveliest things, Gregory." She batted her eyes at him while he made her drink, a mixture of

Scotch, orange juice, sweet vermouth and cherry liqueur. Light on the orange juice.

"Sweet for the sweet."

She laughed, knowing that he only flirted as a matter of course, part of the job. Greg was happily married with twin girls in kindergarten. He exchanged the drink for her ten-dollar bill, and she turned with the chilled glass in her hand, getting ready to head back upstairs and to the dance floor. But a pair of intense eyes pinned her where she stood. Victor Raphael.

He sat at the bar, drinking something from a cocktail glass and looking pleasantly relaxed on the stool. His strong forearms rested easily on the edge of the bar while his eyes held her with the strength of a leash in an iron grip. She forced a casual smile, although butterflies had started a small rebellion in her stomach.

"Mr. Raphael." She nodded in his direction.

"Ms. Davis."

Greg, who had been making his way back to Victor, looked between him and Mella, then abruptly turned to check on his other customers. Victor's attentions, still fierce and predatory, didn't stray from her.

Then the ridiculousness of it all forced her to laugh. They were in a club. She was covered in sweat from dancing the afternoon away, and he was sitting at the bar cool as could be, with what was probably some sort of manly whiskey drink. Their differences couldn't be more apparent.

"You should call me Mella after all this," she said and moved closer to him, despite instincts that screamed at her to run the other way. He wasn't like other men.

She couldn't tease him and walk away and dismiss him from her mind as if he'd never been there.

Victor Raphael nodded. The unforgiving lines of his face and most of his body were wreathed in shadow, but she couldn't mistake the way he stared at her. He didn't say anything, but she forged ahead, anyway.

"And I'll call you Victor."

"If you like." His voice brushed like the finest silk over her skin. Mella shivered.

"I *do* like."

In the half light of the bar, he was even more fierce than at the fund-raiser. All remaining trappings of civility stripped away to leave this brooding shadow man who seemed to have a lot on his mind and wasn't about to change his demeanor simply because someone had wandered into his cave. Because Mella was sometimes foolish, she went further into the beast's lair.

"Why are you drinking alone?" she asked.

"Because I want to." The words should have pushed her away, but she only leaned closer to hear his voice. "The alternative—" he waved vaguely to the party happening above them "—is not much of one."

"Do you want me to leave?"

He tipped his head, appeared to consider it. Appeared to consider many things in that one charged moment. "No. Stay. And let me pay for your next round if you're having one."

The words were so uncharacteristic of the man she'd met at the fund-raiser that she looked down at his glass, wondering at his welcome and just how much he'd had to drink that he was inviting her to stay with him at the bar. Wasn't he the one who'd wanted to get down to business and then go home? Had his drink changed his personality? Although she couldn't talk. This was her third drink, and her blood was just warm enough that she was looser than usual, feeling so good about life that having another drink would take her from nice to naughty. She didn't want that. She didn't want to act that much of a fool with this magnetic stranger. A stranger whom she would be working with very soon.

Mella lifted her glass. "Thanks for the offer, but I'm afraid this is it for me. Although I'm not driving, I don't want to get too blitzed today. I still have some work to get done tonight."

She expected him to ask about her job, what kind of work she did and how long she'd been doing it, maybe even what school she went to. Those were the usual things people asked when they wanted to either dismiss or devour you in the world.

"It's a weekend," Victor said instead. "You should enjoy the rest of your Sunday. Work can wait until an actual workday, can't it?"

She shrugged. In theory, it could. But the reality of owning your own business often didn't allow for workdays versus rest days. But she said none of that. "Maybe you're right."

Sitting next to him, Mella felt that powerful hum of attraction all over her skin, so powerful that it was almost uncomfortable, putting her body in a higher state of awareness than she was used to. Before now, her interactions with men she liked had been all butterfly delight and the uncomplicated steps of a familiar dance. Mella took a sip of her drink to hide her gulping swallow. She felt him follow the movement of the glass to her mouth.

Remnants of the alcohol clung to her top lip. She licked them away and lifted her eyes to his.

"Although I didn't say this before, thank you for donating to the charity this afternoon. The money will go a long way to helping them reach their goal, and the project you'll be working on means a lot to me."

Victor thumbed condensation from the sweating glass in front of him, his mouth curving faintly up. "You should actually be thanking Kingsley. He's the one who put Raphael Design Group up for bid. I had nothing to do with it." His smile turned openly sardonic. "I didn't even know about it."

"Oh." She didn't quite know how to respond to that. Was he pissed off that his friend had volunteered him? Mella started to pull back.

"But—" Victor tapped the smooth surface of the bar near her hand, reaching out to her without touching. "Despite how we got here, I'm glad to help."

"I… I'm glad, too." What kind of friendship did the two men have that something like this was okay?

"It's not as bad as it sounds." Victor's mouth twisted again. "Kingsley just worries about me and my lack of interaction with the larger world." He made a dismissive motion. "Nothing to dwell on." His smile appeared. The nicer one. "So, tell me, what are you drinking?"

Mella blinked, mentally switching to accommodate the abrupt change in topic. *Okay*, she thought. *I can do this.*

Mella told him. "It's sweet and strong, just like me."

A smile darted across his face, briefly crinkling the corners of his eyes. "I've never heard of it."

"Me neither, until recently." Mella put the cocktail glass on the bar and traced a finger through the condensation in random patterns. "I like to try new things," she said. "Sometimes I look online or in menus for a cocktail or food I haven't tried, and then I taste it. If it's good, I enjoy it until it's time to try something else."

"Interesting. Does that habit extend to all areas of your life?"

"Depends on the thing."

"I see. Not everything will suit you, you know." His eyes, a deep agate, grounding and challenging at the same time, held hers in a resolute grip.

Mella's tongue darted out to lick the corner of her lips. "I know. But I want to taste it, sample it, have it again and again until I'm sure it's not for me."

Victor hummed a response, eyes on her mouth, gaze getting warmer by the second. Without asking, she knew what he was thinking. Her lips, his body. A comfortable bed. Maybe even a hidden corner of the bar where he could seduce her lips apart, encourage her to kiss him, to lick and suck whatever he had to offer. Her pulse began a fast and delicious tattoo in her throat.

This, Mella knew. It was flirtation with no consequences. She saw where it was going before it even properly started. A man and a woman in a bar. The spark of attraction. She fell into the moves of the familiar dance, unthinking. Practiced. Despite the electric attraction, unusual and disconcerting, that she felt

for Victor Raphael, she could do casual like this blind-
folded. *If* he was into that kind of thing. She smirked
at the thought.

But things didn't always go the way she expected.

Victor's lashes swept up and his mouth firmed.
"While I am an acquired taste, I'm no one's experi-
ment, Ms. Davis." Without him moving an inch, his
body closed itself off to her. "Taste testers have never
been my preference."

Mella bit her lip and called herself all types of fool.
She *knew* he wasn't a casual man. All she had to do
was look into the swirling brown depths of his eyes
to know that he was a man to drown in, not wade into
and step back when the waves got too close. She sat up
straight on the stool. "Of course, Victor." She picked
up her glass and swallowed a sweet, burning bite of
the drink. "I think it's time for me to get back to my
friends."

His expression didn't change. "Thank you for spend-
ing a bit of your time with me," he said.

"A pleasure." Then she made her escape.

Chapter 2

Mella didn't know how long she had stayed out the night before with her friends, but it had been much too late for someone who had to be at work by 5:00 a.m. Sitting on the patio of the North Beach flagship location of Café Michaela the next morning, she clutched a giant cup of black coffee while going over the previous week's sales and current stock to decide what needed to be reordered.

It was still early, barely 5:30, and she was the only one in the café. Her first employee would arrive within half an hour to begin dealing with the morning rush, but for now, it was just her and the rising sun that seeped into her skin through the thin tank top and shorts she wore.

Mella sat on the patio with her laptop open, the

sound of waves quietly whispering nearby. Her shop was on prime real estate. She'd been lucky to get it for a reasonable price a few years before. She never stopped being thankful for all her blessings, despite the other things in her life that hadn't quite gone her way.

She was sending off an order to her supplier in Ethiopia when her cell phone rang. "Hey." Mella kept her voice low to baby the last remnants of her hangover. She ruffled a hand over her thick hair and stretched out her legs in the sun.

"Good morning, Michaela." Nala Singh laughed at her through the phone. "Either you're trying not to disturb the other early birds, or a killer hangover is about to crack you wide-open." Mella had to smile. Only Nala could make her laugh at herself in this condition.

Since they'd met, the billionaire orphan and jet-setting photographer refused to call Mella by the shortened version of her name, instead insisting, since their names sounded too alike, that she would call Mella by the name her parents gave her.

"What are you doing up so early?" Mella asked.

"I haven't been to sleep yet. But I figured you'd be up doing something very responsible."

"Good guess." Coffee in hand, Mella stepped away from the table and walked to the railing, looking across the paved street to the glimpse of ocean through the bushes. The early-morning sun burned the sky with its incendiary reds and golds, spreading all that lush color through the clouds and over the virgin day. "What did I do to deserve a call so close to your bedtime?"

"Your email, of course. I just read it."

Mella hid her surprise. She'd only sent the email a few hours before while she'd been at Fever. Before the drinks had started to dull her senses. "Good. I think we lucked out with the Raphael Design Group." She ignored the way her stomach fluttered when Nala said the name of Victor's firm. "They have a great reputation, and the projects they've done in Miami and across the States are phenomenal. They're the perfect fit for your Sanctuary project."

"It looks like it. Thanks for sending the links to their website and the *Herald* articles about their work."

"I like to be thorough."

Nala had inherited a mansion from her long-dead parents. It was a place she didn't want to live in and had left to basically rot for years. But then she had the idea to turn it into a nonprofit space for homeless kids, kids who were kicked out of their homes for one reason or another and wanted to stay in school or get jobs but weren't quite able to do it on their own. A sort of semipermanent home for formerly homeless kids. Nala wanted to complete the renovations to the mansion, have a party to celebrate her best friend's marriage and new baby, then turn it over to the kids who wanted to move in.

When Nala told her the idea the night they'd met at a party on Star Island, it instantly captivated Mella. Helping kids who had been abandoned by their parents, people who were supposed to love them no matter what, had resonated with her immediately. She offered to help with the logistics of the mansion's renovations, even finding a firm to deal with the applications to live in the home. The project and what it would eventually do for an underserved part of the city's population made Mella feel she was doing something worthwhile with her life. She was thankful to Nala for giving her that chance.

"I'm hoping the firm would get some good publicity out of this, at the very least," Mella continued. "Victor Raphael has been a good sport about this whole thing, especially since it wasn't even him that put his services up for auction." She explained Kingsley's prank.

Nala snorted. "That sounds like something Kingsley would do. For someone who runs a Fortune 500 company, he has a lot of damn time on his hands."

"You know him?" Mella took another sip of her coffee, then balanced the cup on the railing.

"He's my best-friend-in-law's brother."

Mella laughed, almost choking on her coffee. "What?"

Chuckling, Nala explained their connection, that Kingsley was the older brother to her best friend's husband. "Not complicated at all," she said.

"Of course not."

Mella laughed again and shook her head. It was a small world. "Anyway, Victor's going through with the project, although obviously he doesn't have to." She remembered Victor's melodic and downright sexy voice explaining what his friend had done. "But I sent him an email about Sanctuary this morning. He agreed to meet me at the site later on this week to take a look at what needs to be done."

"Have fun. I know Corinne thinks he's smokin' hot."

Corinne talked to Nala?

"I'm not sure if you can take Corinne's word on something like that. She thinks any man with a pulse is a viable choice."

Laughter snorted at her from the other end of the phone. "Are you saying Victor's not sexy?"

"I'm definitely not saying that..." Mella bit her lip as she remembered Victor sitting at Fever, his furred forearms resting on the bar, the smell of faintly spicy cologne, and beneath that the more natural scent of a man. "He's definitely sexy. But he's too serious. You know I like my men with a sense of humor."

"According to Nichelle, all men have a sense of humor—you just have to tickle them the right way."

"I'm not ready to work that hard," Mella said with a dismissive wave of her hand, although obviously, Nala couldn't see it. But even as she said the words, she wasn't sure she actually believed them. They had been true before she met Victor. She generally liked her men fun and uncomplicated. That way, the affair was light, just like she preferred it. And when it came time for it to end, nobody would cry any disappointed tears or make a scene. But it was a moot point. Victor wasn't a fan of "taste testers."

Her mouth tightened at the phrase he'd used. Not that his reaction hadn't been her fault. What else would a man like that say to someone who basically compared a potential affair with him to having a monthly round of drinks?

Nala's tsk-tsking brought her attention back to their conversation. "Most hard work is worth the reward,

Michaela," Nala said with a teasing lilt. Although Mella hadn't known her long, she knew that Nala didn't necessarily subscribe to that philosophy herself.

"Right." She sipped her coffee, mouth curving in a reluctant smile.

Nala chuckled. "I'll let you get back to your morning routine. But call me if anything comes up about Sanctuary or anything else."

"I will. Thanks."

Mella disconnected the call. Despite what she'd said to Nala, she knew she was already being an idiot. Victor was serious, unlike any of the men she'd dated before. The way he looked at her made her want to both run away from and curl up into him. She didn't want him to laugh at her weak jokes. She didn't want him to smile. She had no interest in changing him into what she liked. She just wanted him to come closer and cover her with all that masculine intensity.

It was raining. An expected rain, but still an annoying one. Victor would rather be in the office for the rest of the day, working on the looming Barcelona project, ordering in lunch and leaving only when it was time to go home. Instead he was in the rain. Granted, he was actually safe and dry in his SUV, but the main point was that he was at a mansion in the farthest reaches of Miami, waiting on a woman whom he didn't quite know what to think of. Michaela Davis. Mella.

She was nothing like he'd thought she would be, yet she was everything his entire being gravitated toward. He'd expected her to be like a butterfly, flitting from one interesting thing to another, laughter always hovering on the curve of her lips. Mella was that, but even more. It seemed that actual *light* emanated from her. A radiance that he longed to bask in even as he tried to convince her, and himself, that her brand of living was not for him.

In that dark corner of the bar, she had been like a glowing curve of bioluminescence that begged for his touch. But no impulse he'd ever gone with had ever gone well in the end. So he pushed her away.

Besides, she was more into Kingsley, anyway. Victor didn't miss the way Mella and his best friend had immediately clicked at the auction. She'd laughed at his jokes, looked up into his face with a smile radiating from her eyes. It wasn't new to him, being looked over in favor of the more outgoing and better-looking Kingsley. But it still sparked something like pain in his chest.

After Fever, he went home to cook, accepting that she wasn't into him, but he found his mind wandering to her. Her smile, the way she tried with a swipe of her hand to push the kinky curls from her face only to have them float back, tickling her nose into an amused wrinkle. It had been an interesting ballet to watch. All beauty and light. Nothing that belonged in his life. Only for someone like Kingsley.

Victor looked at his watch. It was nearly ten thirty. Michaela had been scheduled to meet him at ten. He wondered if she'd canceled the meeting without telling his secretary. No. Though he didn't know her well at all, he figured that wasn't something she would do. Not with this, a project she seemed to care very much about.

But the rain, a light but endless drizzle, made him regret his Italian-leather ankle boots and the pissing away of his morning. Victor glanced at his watch again, remembered that he had a pair of old Timberland boots tucked away in the back of his SUV. He reclined the seat and felt around on the floor of the large truck until his fingers bumped into the hard leather of his boots. He was tying the laces of the second boot when he saw a flash of light green, a Fiat convertible making its way up the long driveway through the rain.

The small car came up the circle drive and swerved neatly around him to park in front of his SUV. A sticker on the back of the ridiculously tiny car read My Other Car is a Motorcycle.

The car's taillights flickered out, and the driver's-side door opened. Purple rain boots splashed into the standing water. Black knee socks, bare legs, then a small denim skirt that clung to curvaceous hips. Mella was wearing a light green T-shirt that said "I didn't claw my way up the food chain to eat vegetables." A clear umbrella popped open before her head emerged fully from the car. Her hair was damp around her face, and she was smiling.

"Hi, Victor." She waved the umbrella at him, then snapped it shut after gauging the intensity of the rain with one upraised palm, not bothering to apologize for being late. "Come on."

After a moment's pause, he left the safety of the truck, locking the Mercedes with a click of the remote. "It's raining," he said once he was at her side. She smelled like soft mint candy.

"I know. Isn't it nice?" Mella unlocked the massive front door and wiped off her boots on the mat before stepping into the house. Despite the overgrown mess of the front yard and the large fountain that was crumbled and needed fixing, the inside of the house was immaculate. It smelled of fresh paint and furniture polish. The banister to the wooden staircases on both sides of the foyer gleamed from a recent cleaning. There was no furniture. "They did a great job fixing this place up," she said. "You should have seen it a few months ago." Her voice echoed in the empty space.

There was something about her, standing in the entryway of a deserted house, that he found dangerous. The whole look of her was inviting, the tilt of her head, the scent of rain and tangerine shampoo that sweetened the air around her, the clinging invitation of the short denim skirt. Victor wanted to move closer, so he stayed in the doorway. If he were Kingsley, he wouldn't want a man who hadn't had sex in over two years sniffing after the next woman to end up in his bed.

"We're here to look at the grounds," he said carefully, wanting very much to wrap his hands around her hips and test the feel of her. "But the rain makes it too difficult to see what needs to be done. We can come back another time when it's dry."

Mella looked at him with her big eyes from under her big hair, her head slightly tilted as she smiled. "We're here. We might as well look at the grounds now. A wet lawn looks pretty much the same as a dry one."

When he didn't move, she shrugged and walked toward him, coming back out of the house. He stepped out of her way before she could reach him. "But you're right about one thing, though. Why go through the house when the exterior is all you need to see?" Mella hooked her umbrella over one arm and looped the other through his. It was only his surprise and her boldness that allowed her to tug him around the wide wraparound porch, down a flight of marble stairs and out to the overgrown backyard.

The rain was light as a woman's fingers on his head and cheeks, its touch cool but soothing after the heat of the morning. Despite his earlier complaints, Victor breathed in the smell of the rain and of the green grass under his feet with a minute shudder of pleasure. This was another part of his job he loved—wading into the disorder of nature and finding harmony in it.

The grounds were large, but he'd worked on larger. The grass was overgrown, the weeds bold enough to take over nearly every inch of free space, leaving room for occasional sprouts of wildflowers and dandelions. A small orchard of mango trees lined the back of the property while a high garden maze, at least seven feet high, that had lost nearly all of its rigid form, took up nearly half the space. He would have to fix that.

"It looks daunting," she said. "What do you think?"

Watching her with the wind flinging her wet hair at her cheeks, her hands on her hips and the wet curve of her smiling mouth, Victor thought he just might be in trouble. Big trouble.

He surveyed the property, the back first and then the front, walking around the acre plus of overgrown land, dried grass, wild fruit trees and out of control weeds. Juggling his umbrella so his iPad wouldn't get wet, he took notes and pictures, briefly sketching ideas of what he wanted to do. Mella sat on the steps as he worked, having finally opened her umbrella, eyes taking in the gloomy morning, the heavy clouds, while Victor walked through the untamed gardens.

While he worked, he felt her eyes on him, assessing. Her gaze made him vaguely uneasy, but there was something in him that enjoyed her attention, the focus of such a striking and unpredictable woman who couldn't look away from him.

Unlike most people, she didn't take out a cell phone, book or some electronic device to pass the time. She simply watched him and the rest of her world with her large and devouring stare.

When he was finished with the front and back of the house, he joined her on the stairs with his own open umbrella. Rain tapped the umbrella as he held it over both their heads. She folded hers closed and put it at her feet.

"What's the verdict?" she asked.

"It's a beautiful property," he said. "It'll be even more beautiful when I'm finished with it."

He took out his notes and shared his ideas on the space. Trim up the English maze, install a fountain, transplant the fruit trees to another part of the yard, put in a paved walking path winding through the entire front and back of the mansion.

Victor kept his language as straightforward as possible, making sure the entire process was transparent. As he spoke, he noticed her frowning more than once, but she waited until he was finished to voice her concerns.

"I don't like any of it," she said.

Victor had to mentally repeat what she said to make sure he wasn't misunderstanding her. Mella shook her head and reached over to tap the surface of his iPad, enlarging the image. Despite the layers of clothes between them, he felt her warmth, the way the muscles of her arm moved.

"The fruit trees should stay where they are. The kids would love to have their own mango trees in the backyard instead of going through the garden to get them." Her breath brushed against his neck as she spoke, her attention completely focused on the notes he laid out on the tablet. "They're for fun and food, not just to look good. And the English maze—" she actually put up air quotes with the closest thing to a sneer he'd ever seen on her face "—I want that to look more natural. Those mazes in English movies are boring. You can still leave it a maze, but nothing so rigid. Give the plants some room to breathe. Leave the flowers that are accidentally growing together. I don't like rectangular plants, and I don't think the kids will, either."

The longer she spoke, the more he frowned until he swore his forehead had folded in on itself. Just who was the professional here? "You don't like any of *my* suggestions?" He made it a question because he couldn't believe it.

"Sorry, that's not quite true." She grinned at him as if she was about to pay him the biggest compliment. "I like that type of buffalo grass you suggested. It won't need too much maintenance after it takes hold."

"Listen…"

But she was already standing up and walking out into the rain with her umbrella. Her purple boots splashed in the puddles and squished in the grass. She stood with the closed umbrella, its curved handle draped over her arm. Mella stared out into the wide yard, her breath blowing out the drops of water falling in front of her mouth.

"This place is beautiful and natural and should feel like a home. The garden is overgrown, but that's what makes it pretty, don't you think?"

He didn't tell her what he really thought.

"The grounds just need a little grooming, not a complete overhaul." She turned to him, and Victor felt his breath catch. Damn, she was…

"Frustrating."

She drew up to every inch of her five feet nothing. "What?"

"You can't have it both wild and civilized, Ms. Davis. You have to choose. Having it both ways just doesn't make sense, and it's not possible. I'm telling you the best way to do this."

"Well, I'm telling you it *is* possible. I'm trusting you to perform what's apparently a miracle—" she lifted her eyebrows at him, mouth aggressively smiling, all teeth and little warmth "—and give Nala and the kids exactly what they want."

"Right now, you're the one saying what *you* want.

Why, when your opinion, as you've just said, doesn't matter in this equation?"

She was clenching her teeth so hard Victor thought they would crack. "You should assume what I'm telling you is exactly what Nala wants. Create something beautiful that won't make the kids feel like they're living in a showplace. It's a home, not somewhere they're made to feel like they don't belong."

Frustration bubbled up in his chest, but he tamped it down. "All right," he said. "All right. Let's start again, shall we?"

Her jaw relaxed, and her smile became more natural. The sight of it loosened a tightness he hadn't known was in his chest. She grinned up at him, a small ray of sunshine glowing beneath the heavy gray skies.

"Oh, good." Her smile widened.

He was so screwed.

Chapter 3

Mella shouldn't have touched him. But she thought if she put their flesh together, casually, as she'd done with any other man in the past, it would be nothing. That she would get past the foolish notion that touching Victor would be significant. But it had been much worse than she thought.

On the porch of the mansion, she looped her arm through his and felt shivers run through her body, tiny seismic events jolting through her and making her deeply regret the impulsive move. His skin on hers was exactly the shock to the system she had been expecting. And more. He smelled like something she wanted to put on her body. A favorite blanket, an old T-shirt, Christmas socks that felt perfect while she lay by the fire. Even now, after he'd driven off to his office or wherever he needed to be at one o' clock on a Thursday afternoon, her entire side tingled from where she'd been pressed against him. The core of her felt like it had been flung about on a roller coaster. Stupid. She had been utterly stupid.

Mella sat in her car with the windows up, steam fogging up the interior as her thoughts ran completely away from her.

This is pointless, she thought. *I need to get out of here.*

With a shuddering sigh, she started the engine and roared her little car down the long driveway. The tires hissed through the rain, windshield wipers thudding back and forth across the glass.

There was work to do at the café, but she didn't feel like dealing with any of it. Not with the awareness of Victor Raphael riding so close to the surface of her skin. Mella just drove. She didn't realize where she was going until she pulled into Mary McLeod Bethune Park. The small Coconut Grove park lay between two roads, one open to vehicular traffic and the other closed to everyone but the long line of motorcycles doing the charity ride for pelican protection and conservation.

Her aunt Jessamyn, who didn't give a damn about pelicans but used any excuse she could to travel with other bikers, was on the ride. Around one thirty, she and the other riders were supposed to take a break at the park to eat and stretch their legs before continuing north to Deerfield Beach. If Mella had thought about it, she would have ridden her own motorcycle to link up with her aunt, but the anticipation of meeting with

Victor Raphael that morning had made basic thought processes impossible.

It was still raining, and her hair was already wet. The rain jacket she pulled from her car kept the rest of her mostly dry, though. Her boots squelched in the grass as she crossed the manicured green to the other side of the park and to the line of motorcycles. She took out her phone and called her aunt.

"Are you still at the park?"

Her aunt immediately answered in her gravelly voice. "Yeah. By the statue of the old girl. One of the shaded picnic benches." In the background, Mella could hear other voices and the occasional grumble of a motorcycle.

Mella waded through the crowd of bikers, fifty at least, and easily found her aunt in the roundabout, her bike parked near the eight-foot bronze statue of Mary McLeod Bethune. Her aunt straddled her big purple Harley while she chatted up another biker, a man with a handlebar mustache and most of his muscled chest bare under an open leather vest.

Even in a crowd like this, her aunt stood out. Almost unnaturally beautiful, she'd gotten even more striking in her middle age. She had long ago traded her sleek pantsuits and blazers for jeans, biker boots and the occasional tuxedo when she was in the mood. Today, she wore her mostly salted hair in two big French braids with the ends curled like snails at her shoulders. The freckles on her sand-colored cheeks glistened under the steadily falling raindrops.

As Mella came closer, her aunt's companion gave

her a fist bump, then wandered off. Aunt Jess waved at Mella. "I didn't expect to see you here, honey."

"I didn't expect me, either." Mella made a face, irritated with herself now that she was officially running to her aunt as if someone had stolen her lunch money.

"What's wrong, Michaela?" Her aunt's forehead wrinkled in concern.

But even though she'd run halfway across the city to see the woman who had raised her, she wasn't ready to talk about it yet. *It* being whatever the hell Victor was doing to her.

"I'm not sure," Mella finally said. "Maybe I'm just feeling restless." She rubbed a hand over her face.

But Aunt Jess wasn't buying her helpless act. "You're a terrible liar, Michaela. But I'll wait." She got off her bike and pulled a minicooler from her saddlebag, then pointed Mella toward an empty picnic bench under a nearby banyan tree offering some protection from the light rain.

Aunt Jess unpacked two sandwiches, two bottles of water and a bag of potato chips from the cooler. "Eat. It's lunchtime, and I doubt you've made the time to get something."

"I was going to stop by Gillespie's on the way back to the café." But she took a sandwich anyway, one of her favorites her aunt made with turkey, rye bread and raw kale. The wasabi mayo burned sweetly as she chewed her first bite. "This is good."

"Don't talk with your mouth full," her aunt chided, but she was smiling. She opened the other sandwich and nudged the bag of kettle chips closer to Mella's hand.

When she was very young, Aunt Jessamyn had been one of Mella's favorite adults to be around. Her aunt liked the same movies Mella did, cooked the best food and liked to do different things from the rest of her family, including her own parents. Although Aunt Jessamyn had a kid of her own, Shaun, she often acted like a child herself, laughed loud and long in public, impulsively took Mella and Shaun on trips to Disney World and learned to ride motorcycles just because. She loved doing things for the experience of them, and that was one of the things Mella had always enjoyed about her favorite aunt and her mother's only sister.

The three aunts on her father's side were boring. It just seemed natural that after Mella's parents died when she was eight, Aunt Jessamyn was the one to take her in. She'd loved her parents and missed them every day, but she was glad she had Aunt Jess.

"How's the ride going?" Mella asked after chewing a mouthful of chips.

"Decent enough. It would be good if this rain let up, but it's not too bad. Watching out for the fool drivers cutting up in this weather is a decent distraction from thinking about Shaun."

Mella nodded. She'd noticed the date, nearly four years to the day Shaun had been sent away to begin his ten years behind bars for vehicular manslaughter. Her aunt was hurting. Mella reached across the table and squeezed her hand.

"You saw him this week?" she asked.

Her aunt nodded. "Yesterday. He's in such bad shape." She pressed her lips together, her face a mask of pain. "I'm not sure he'll last in that place if he doesn't get paroled. Every time we talk, he tells me he's sorry for what he did and wishes he could take it all back."

"I know," Mella said. "We all wish that."

But they didn't live in a world where wishes came true and felons got released just because their mothers were sad.

When Shaun was only twenty and in college, he'd been dumb enough to get behind the wheel after a few too many drinks. The crazy thing was he'd done it so many times before that he hadn't even thought twice about doing it again. Or at least that's what he'd told Mella when she visited him in prison.

That night, he'd had too many drinks and didn't notice the stop sign until he'd plowed through it in his SUV and T-boned a little white sedan. The man in the car hadn't survived. And although her aunt, through her tears of anger and disappointment, had hired some of the best lawyers in Miami, Shaun had still been sent away for ten years. That was a long time to be without your child.

Shaun had done some crazy things before the accident, partying hard with kids with more money and less responsibilities, kids whose parents lived in a higher tax bracket and played outside the boundaries of the law, knowing that their parents could get them out of trouble if necessary.

Mella tried to warn him about what could happen, but he didn't listen. Then he was in jail, and his so-called friends disappeared from his life as if they'd never been there. Mella and Aunt Jess had been try-

ing to pick up the pieces over the years. And now that
he'd served his minimum sentence and was eligible
for parole, Mella and her aunt crossed their fingers
that the prison system would let him go. Shaun was
only twenty-four. He had spent so many of his prime
years in prison.

"Do you need some company tonight?" Mella asked.
"I can make us that lasagna you like."

Although her aunt lived in a decent-sized house on
Key Biscayne and often had her housekeeper make
meals for her for the week, Mella knew she'd appreciate the offer.

Her aunt nodded. "That would be nice." She balled
up the empty sandwich bag in a delicate fist while
Mella finished the last of the chips. "A vegetarian lasagna?"

Mella shook her head in disgust. "Hell no! What
do I look like?"

Her aunt chuckled. "Just checking. You've been
hanging out a lot with that Nala woman."

"It's just work, Aunt Jess. Besides, you should be
worrying about her other habits rubbing off on me, not
the fact that she doesn't eat meat." Nala loved to party,
loved to travel to places that weren't the safest and had
a wicked collection of knives in her Wynwood loft.

Her aunt made a noise that was all doubt. "That girl
is a bad influence."

"She's fine. Just because she doesn't work doesn't
make her a bad influence."

"Idle hands, Michaela."

Mella grinned. It was funny that the only people

who called her Michaela were her aunt and Nala, the girl she disapproved of so much. "She's nice. Once you meet her you'll see."

The sound of a whistle pierced the rainy afternoon. A woman stood on a picnic table at the far end of the park waving a green flag. The whistle between her lips shrieked again.

"Break time is over." Her aunt threw the remnants of lunch in the nearby trash can. "Do you want to do the rest of the ride with me?" she asked. "It's only another couple of hours, then we head back into the city."

Mella didn't even have to think about it. The bike ride would be a distraction from her own obsessions. Specifically the one that wore Victor Raphael's face. "Sure. I can catch up on my work when I get back."

At the bike, she took her aunt's spare helmet, hitched up her already short skirt and climbed on the back of the big, rumbling Harley. The seat was damp under her butt, and the bike's rumble rattled her teeth. The world beyond the screen of her helmet was still rainy, still cloudy, but it felt good to have her aunt near her, even if they were both carrying their separate worries.

"Lead on, warrior princess," she called to her aunt, her voice muffled behind the helmet.

"That's warrior queen to you, girl!" Her aunt opened up the throttle, and they were off.

The Miami Heat was losing the basketball game, but Victor was having a good time, anyway. He was grateful to Kingsley—again—for dragging him out into the world. He had a lot to do at home—cook, work out, look over the draft of the grant request his sister, Vivian, had sent him. But a phone call from Kingsley had him sitting on the courtside, watching Dwyane Wade try to get his team back on top.

"This might be a lost cause," Kingsley said. But he sounded disgustingly cheerful over the fact.

Kingsley spent more of his time people-watching and answering texts from his little sister than paying attention to what was happening on the court. The game was good, though. The Pistons were putting on a good show and making the Heat work for every score they got.

"Depends on what cause you're talking about." Victor swallowed the last of his sparkling water. "I know *I'm* having fun watching them get burned for a change. Keeps them humble."

Victor looked away from the court when Kingsley nudged him.

"Hey, isn't that the auction honey?" He jerked his head across the court where a trio of women jumped to their feet and cheered along with the crowd to the sudden three-pointer by one of the Heat.

Yes, it was definitely Mella. No need to ask Kingsley who he was talking about. She was with her friends from the auction. This time all three women were dressed more casually. Mella wore a white T-shirt under a bright yellow blazer, and tight jeans clung to her exquisite body. She was as distracting as ever, exchanging high fives with her two friends and laughing in a way that made him wonder what the joke was.

He hadn't seen her since the afternoon they'd looked

over the grounds of Sanctuary together. But that didn't mean he hadn't been thinking about her. Often. And at the most inconvenient times. Those thoughts made him feel like he was cheating with his friend's girl. Kingsley never explicitly expressed an interest in Mella, but Victor could see the writing on the wall. They were going to end up together, and he was just going to end up looking stupid.

People were jumping to their feet, whistling, applauding and flagging down the hot dog guys. Halftime.

"Let's go see what the ladies are up to." Kingsley stood up. He was apparently anxious to go talk to Mella.

But Victor couldn't blame him. If he had been the one Mella was interested in, he would already be over there staking his claim, "taste tester" or not. Once she had a taste, maybe she'd discover he was what she craved. He swallowed at the thought. "You go ahead," he said. "I'll just chill here."

He couldn't bear watching them together from up close. He didn't want it to be a repeat of their visit to Fever. Not only had it been torture to watch Mella dance with Kingsley and share flirtatious smiles with him, it had also been a social situation he wasn't quite prepared for. Hundreds of people had crowded him with their sweat and expectations. Women approached him. Men sized him up as competition. The thought of it made his skin crawl a little. But later, when Mella had unexpectedly found him at the downstairs bar, he hadn't minded as much. There, he'd almost managed to convince himself he was the one she wanted. She'd been a warm and brilliant thing, tempting him with the wet stroke of tongue across her lips, the low hum of her voice as she leaned closer to him at the bar.

He remembered wanting to tug open the buttons of the tiny shirt she wore and just stare at her nipples until they stiffened and ached for his touch. She'd talked about tasting that night, and *God*, he'd wanted to taste. Later in bed, he'd had particularly vivid dreams.

In the seat next to him, Kingsley glanced at his phone, then shoved it back in his pocket. "You know, not every woman's waiting around the corner with a shank. Metaphorically speaking."

Victor winced at the idea that he might be talking about Mella. Was Kingsley really that into her?

But Victor tried to play it off. "Are you saying that with your big head, or the little one?"

Like him, Kingsley had had his share of ruthless women in his life. The only woman he'd been interested in and that actually seemed decent turned out to be his brother's current wife. She was a woman who seemed ruthless on the outside, all vicious high heels and dry humor. Underneath it all, though, she was a version of sweet. But it turned out she'd also had a thing for Kingsley's brother, Wolfe, for years before the two of them finally hooked up.

"Don't be a dick, Vic." Kingsley grinned at the rhyme, and what he obviously thought was a good joke. "There's nothing wrong with entertaining a beautiful woman or two for the afternoon. But if you want, I'll pass along your hellos."

Just for the afternoon? Mella deserved more than that, if that was what she wanted.

Victor shrugged the tightness from his shoulders. He needed to pull his head out of his ass exactly right now. *Stop. Thinking. About. Her.* But from the corner of his eye, he couldn't help but notice her wild, haloing hair and the graceful bow of her back as she threw her whole body into a laugh. She and her friends had attracted the attentions of the other people around them, especially the men. Victor winced again.

Although he didn't want to see Kingsley with Mella, he wasn't exactly eager to be in that social of a crowd. Part of him had always thought there was something wrong with him for not wanting to socialize much. Hell, even his parents enjoyed getting out more than he did. Being in crowds didn't torture him, per se, but when he was expected to interact with the hoard, his comfort level dropped into the basement. His sister said he had mild social anxiety. Victor just thought he was selective about the people and situations he exposed himself to.

All around him, people were chattering, gobbling down hot dogs, dancing to the loud music coming from the speakers. No one looked at him. No one seemed to expect anything from him. He was cool with that.

"Go ahead," he said to Kingsley. "I'll be right here enjoying the view."

Kingsley hesitated, a split-second pause, before he glanced again at his phone then stood up. "I'll be back."

"All right, Ahnald."

Kingsley chuckled as he walked away.

While his friend made his way toward Mella and
her friends, Victor leaned back in his seat and watched
the action in the stands. A tall guy who looked like a
pro ball player joined Mella and her friends, no doubt
drawn to their collective vivacity and beauty. Victor
didn't recognize him, but that wasn't saying much.

Mella's friends, though, seemed immediately star-
struck, flirting with the tall guy and then with Kingsley, who'd walked into their gathering with enviable
ease. When his friend got to the women, they looked
like a blessing had fallen on them straight from heaven.
One of Mella's friends—he couldn't tell them apart—
amped up the charm on the ball player while the other
claimed Kingsley. Despite the attempted pairing up,
Mella never lost the attentions of the ball player or
Kingsley. Victor didn't bother guessing what they were
talking about. Would Kingsley mention him?

That question answered itself when Mella, talking
to Kingsley, looked up and straight across the rows of
seats to Victor. She waved at him and smiled before
turning back to her conversation.

He didn't take his eyes off Mella. She seemed to flirt
readily with Kingsley, meeting his eyes and laughing
at his jokes. But she kept her hands to herself, unlike
her friends. Someone he hadn't noticed before made
her way toward Mella and Kingsley carrying a tray of
food. Victor knew her. Nala Singh. A close friend of
the Diallo family. She was dressed all in black, with
her straightened hair braided into a crown on top of
her head.

When Mella noticed her, she squealed in happiness

and grabbed her in a tight hug before taking the tray. With the food there, Mella paid the men barely half the attention she gave them before, digging into the sandwich and fries as if it was her last meal.

So, she liked food. He had a moment's thought of feeding her something he made in his kitchen, seducing her with sweet meats and spicy sauces, aromatic breads and crisp fruit, before he reined himself in. *Kingsley wants her*, he told himself. *Back up*.

But he still watched her. Across the stands, Mella devoured her food, only occasionally taking part in the conversations going on around her. Nala hugged Kingsley and laughed at something he said, playfully tapped at his stomach with a closed fist. They stood close together, like friends, but there was no flirtation between them.

Maybe, he thought with sudden desperation, maybe he and Mella could become friends like that. Maybe it would be no problem to work with her on the Sanctuary project after all, their differences over the project's vision aside.

Just before the game started again, Kingsley came back to Victor's side. "You missed a good time," he said.

"I doubt that," Victor muttered. But he glanced back at Mella one more time before giving his attention back to the court.

After the game and drinks with Kingsley, he went home. Alone. At his desk, he pulled up his notes for the Sanctuary renovation. He'd planned on turning it over to one of the junior architects at the firm, someone who didn't have very much going on and was essentially apprenticing.

But he pulled the details from the digital outbox and sent an email to the junior architect to let him know he would handle the project after all. On the morning at the mansion, the morning it rained and her purple boots sank into the wet grass next to his Timberland boots, Victor had felt overwhelmed by his attraction for her. And also annoyed with her as a client. The annoyance, and loyalty to Kingsley, had won, and he had decided not to deal with her more than strictly necessary.

But with one look across that basketball court, he realized things didn't have to be so black-and-white. Her light was a seductive thing. Even though she had been flirting and showing off her incandescent beauty for other men, he hadn't been able to look away. Until he met Mella, Victor didn't know that people like her, innately beautiful and full of life, existed. It couldn't hurt to have friends like that, right?

But that night before falling into his bed, he thought of her. And not as a friend. Remembering the bright laughter in her face and the temptation of her body, it didn't take long for him to imagine what her mouth would feel like under his…her long legs wrapped around his waist as he sipped the laughter from her lips…

Chapter 4

Of the three European-style cafés Mella owned, the one on North Beach, her first, was her favorite. Café Michaela, with its bright yellow awning stretched over half a dozen sidewalk tables, sat across the street from a path leading to the beach. The café was usually busy with beachgoers in their bikinis or swim shorts grabbing a sandwich or coffee on the way to or from the water. There were also the college student and remote-working regulars who plugged themselves into a power outlet first thing in the morning, ordered coffee and tea all day and didn't leave until just before the café closed. It was a good business.

When Mella opened the first café eight years before, she'd only been armed with business school sense, her natural optimism and the rest of the small inheritance from her parents. But her business gamble paid off beyond her wildest dreams. After opening two other locations, things were going better than ever. Her customers were loyal, and her employees some of the friendliest she'd had the pleasure of working with. The life she had was a damn nice one, and a day didn't pass when she wasn't grateful for it.

At sunrise, she sat at her favorite sidewalk table and watched the day unfold. Already, she'd contacted all three of her managers, sent off her orders and sent messages to the recent interviewees she wanted to hire. It was with a sense of accomplishment that she opened her laptop and checked her email for the second time that morning.

One of the first messages in her inbox, after the invitation to try Viagra risk free for thirty days, was a message from Victor. It was sent at four o'clock that morning, an hour before her alarm went off.

Ms. Davis
Good morning. I've attached the plans for the Sanctuary project. If you'd like to talk further about the changes, you can reach me at the number in my email signature. Let me know your thoughts.

Mella smiled, imagining how it must have pained him to write the last sentence. He didn't want to know what she thought. He just wanted to complete the project Kingsley had signed him up for. She wondered if he had turned the entire grounds of the mansion into a giant English maze with instructions for her to get lost.

That thought shouldn't have been funny, especially since he obviously hated being told what to do, but she laughed anyway.

Seeing him at the basketball game a few days before had been a delicious, multilayered pleasure. Sweet and bitter, both. At first, when Kingsley told her Victor was at the game, too, her pulse had thundered at the thought of talking with him again. She looked across the rows of stadium seats and saw Victor sitting in the midst of the crowd, stoic and self-contained, as if he had no connection with the people around him and wanted to keep it that way. She'd wanted to hear his rumbling cat's voice close to her ear, feel that electric shock of their fingers touching. But she also didn't want to intrude. Mella knew what it was like to have people encroach on her space when she wasn't ready or willing for them to.

And so she'd smiled and waved and snuck looks at him for the rest of the game, devouring the wide stretch of his shoulders under the black T-shirt, the loving curve of fabric over his crotch. That night, she had woken from dreams that left her sticky and wet. Mella squirmed in her seat in the café and tried to refocus on work.

She clicked on Victor's email attachment, prepared to be disappointed again. But after looking at the plans, she grinned with pleasure and surprise. The schematics he'd sent were…perfect. It was as if he reached into her mind and plucked out every important thing she and Nala had imagined together. It was beautiful.

Her hand hovered over her cell phone to call him,

but then she looked down and saw the time. If he went to bed after four, he probably wouldn't appreciate her waking him at six, no matter the reason. Instead of calling Victor, she forwarded the email to Nala and asked what she thought. Less than an hour later, she received a reply from Nala laced with smiley faces.

This is damn good! Make sure to thank him properly for this. I don't think anyone else could have made something so perfect. Awesome work!!

Mella rolled her eyes. Thank him properly? The only thanks he probably wanted was to be left alone. But the more she thought about it, the more she second-guessed herself. After mentally going back and forth for nearly an hour, she finally settled on showing her gratitude with lunch. After making an appointment with his secretary, Mella showed up at his office with nothing but her good will and an invitation to eat with her at one of the best restaurants in town.

She waited outside his office, playing "Words With Friends" with Aunt Jess and occasionally checking her email. She'd just scored with *quizzical* when the secretary, a soft-looking woman with a thick New York accent and bright red lipstick, told her it was her turn to see the big boss. Mella thanked her with a smile and knocked once on Victor's door before stepping inside.

"Good afternoon." He stood to greet her with a nod and firm handshake. "It was a surprise to see you on my calendar, Ms. Davis."

He looked, in a word, delicious. Black suited him.

That must be why he wore it all the time. The color was perfect against his copper skin and made her fingers itch to touch him.

"I hope it's a good surprise," she said with a grin. Her reaction to him grew stronger every time she saw him. Not good. "And it's Mella, remember?"

"Everything about you—" he said after a moment "—is impossible to forget."

Mella blinked in surprise at his words, felt slightly better when he seemed discomfited, too, as if he hadn't meant to say them. Everything about him in that moment was touch and retreat, as though he wanted her but didn't want to want her. It was maddening. Victor stepped back behind his desk with a frown. "What can I do for you today?"

"It's not what you can do for me, Victor." She deliberately used his first name. "It's what I want to do for you."

His eyebrow rose. "Please, enlighten me."

"It would please me very much to take you out to lunch," she said. "My treat. To thank you for the wonderful job you did on Sanctuary. I can't wait for the landscape work to start."

He looked at her as if she was speaking an unfamiliar language.

She tried again. "So will you have lunch with me?"

Victor's chair squeaked when he leaned forward and braced his arms on the edge of his desk. The flex of his arms against the wood reminded Mella of the afternoon at Fever when they'd talked almost intimately in the shadows of the bar, flirtation and possibility flickering between them. He linked his fingers, then looked up at her with a face nearly empty of expression.

"Apologies, but I won't be able to," he said.

Mella swallowed her surprising disappointment. "Why?"

He sat back, looking almost shocked that she questioned him. "I have another appointment."

She resisted the urge to push him even more, ask him to dinner instead. But even she had her limits. "That's too bad."

"Yes, it is. Maybe some other time."

It was hard for her to read him. Did "some other time" mean "never in our collective lifetime" or "maybe later on in the week"? She was so busy dissecting his words that she didn't notice him get up from the desk, only felt the light pressure of his hand on the small of her back—an odd intimacy after his dismissal from moments before. She turned and he took a slow step back.

"Some other time would work well for me," he said. "We can have a friendly lunch."

Victor was so close that she could've counted his eyelashes. Mella shivered, something telling her to back away from him. But she stepped closer instead, claiming the space he'd just abandoned. His eyes opened wider, a slight flaring of his pupils that made Mella want to grab his shirt and pull him closer, but she clenched her fists instead, willing herself to move out of his personal space and leave, because that was what he wanted, right?

"Ms. Davis." The way he said her last name was, strangely, like an invitation to sex. Low and dark and seductive, like she imagined his bedroom to be, the danger and pleasure of him tugging her deep. Mella licked her lips. And tasted him. Between one breath and the next, he leaned down into her space and pressed his lips to hers in a hot connection of flesh that made her tremble. Maybe it was a mistake. Maybe he hadn't meant—

But his tongue traced the seal of her lips, and all thoughts of accidental kisses dropped out of her brain. Breath fluttered from her. Victor tasted softer than he looked. The shape of his mouth that she'd memorized by sight had struck her as a hard and unforgiving line. But that mouth on hers was soft as a dream.

The contradiction burned a trail of desire from her lips to her lap. She whimpered and curled her fingers into the lapels of his blazer. That sound set off something in him. He growled into her and grabbed her hands, trapped them behind her back in a way that arched her back and tightened her nipples, hardened and painful, against his chest. His mouth opened over hers with hot and hungry intent, obliterating the feeling of softness.

Now Victor kissed her like she thought he would. An uncompromising entrance into her mouth, licking her lips, tongue flicking along hers to caress and waken and seduce. The ravenous movement of his mouth over her own stroked sounds from the back of her throat. She wanted to touch him. *Needed* to. Mella tried to pull back.

"Let me go!" She gasped the words against his mouth, and he instantly released her.

Yes!

She dove into him the instant her hands were free,

sinking her fingers into the fabric of his dress shirt, kissing him back as relentlessly as he'd kissed her. He immediately got on board, a low rumble of approval when his hands were free to grip her hips and pull her tight against him. He was hard as steel against her belly.

Mella shivered and moved with him, their bodies snaking instinctively together. Her usual teasing way of handling an attraction like this fell away in the face of how urgent it felt to touch him, the promise of electricity in that first meeting fulfilled in the flickers of feeling darting through her body, every place they touched firing a need inside her that made her moan shamelessly.

The sound of their kisses was wet and urgent in the room. The intimate noises scoured over Mella's flesh, writhed her against him. She raked her nails up the back of his neck, to his hair. His hips jerked against hers, and he growled again.

Oh...

She drew her fingers over his head again, sinking in her nails with every pass. It was like pulling a switch in him. He gripped her even tighter, pushed her back against the front of his desk. The wood pressed into the backs of her thighs. The wetness between her legs became even more so with the rough slant of his mouth over hers.

"Mr. Raphael, your next appointment is on the way." The phone's intercom made Mella jump. Victor steadied her, calmed her as he pulled slowly away, his mouth wet from their kisses. He licked his lips, eyes falling to her chest where her nipples felt painfully hard through her blouse. Mella's pulse hammered madly in her throat.

She drew a deep breath and straightened her blouse.

"I'll let you get back to your day," she said, willing her voice to be steady.

On trembling legs, she moved away from his desk and walked toward the door. She took another deep breath and brushed a hand over the front of her skirt before reaching for the door handle. Mella paused again and looked over her shoulder to find Victor's back to her. But she didn't have to wait long before he turned. Her eyes immediately dropped to the front of his slacks, to the arousal he didn't try to hide. He put his hands in his pockets, wincing briefly. If she didn't know better, she'd say he looked stricken, as if he'd just done something he regretted. But did she know better?

Victor cleared his throat, looking serious all over again. "I'll see you soon, Ms. Davis."

She couldn't help but laugh. "The next time, if you don't call me Mella, I'll have to do something rash."

He tilted his chin up, a faint line between his eyes, seeming curious despite whatever made him pull so completely away from her just seconds before. "Like what?"

"Like crawl into your lap and kiss you until all you can remember is my name."

"Oh." His eyebrow did that arching thing again, face held carefully blank. "Very well. See you soon. Mella."

She threw another grin over her shoulder at him,

all bravado. "See you." Then she opened his door and left the temptation of him behind until another day.

Victor stared at the door after it closed behind Mella, his pulse pounding loudly in his ears.

Goddammit!

He drooped abruptly back against his desk, then shot upright, remembering how Mella had felt pressed against it, her breathy moans, how badly he'd wanted to push up her skirt and feel if she was as wet as she sounded.

Shit.

He shouldn't have touched her, shouldn't have kissed her. But he licked his lips, stroking the tingle her taste left behind, unable to help himself. The poisonous cocktail of guilt and arousal swirling in his blood damn near made him breathless. He had to talk to Kingsley about what he'd done. This couldn't go on.

He was trying to stay away from Mella, but she was even more intoxicating than he'd imagined. Just one kiss and his body had gone into overdrive, ready to slide inside hers and wring more of those erotic noises from her mouth. The arousal was hard and heavy in his belly, and it wasn't just because he hadn't had a woman in years. He pressed a hand to the front of his pants to relieve the ache, but the touch only made things worse. He wanted *her* hands on him, *her* mouth.

But those weren't things he could have. He had to call Kingsley. Now.

A chime from his cell phone interrupted his thoughts. He cleared his throat and plucked the phone from its corner on his desk after glancing briefly at the caller ID. "Are you in the building?" he asked.

"Yes and you better be ready." His sister's voice rang loud and clear through the phone. "I'm not in the mood to mess around. I'm starving." Her last word trailed off in an exaggerated whine. Victor shook his head, smiling despite his scattered thoughts and his hard—

"I'm walking out of my office now." True to his word, he made sure his wallet was in his back pocket and shrugged off his blazer to hold in front of him while his body got itself back under control. He left his office, still on the phone. "See you in a few."

His secretary, Ursula, was on her computer when he walked up to her desk. Her red-tipped fingers tapped fluidly over the keys even as she looked away from the screen to see what he wanted. "I'm leaving now. Even if I'm not back in an hour, you can leave for lunch."

She nodded and tossed him a smile. "Have fun." At times, Victor felt lucky to have Ursula. She was the most efficient woman he'd ever met. As cheerful as he was serious, she instantly made everyone who came to his office comfortable. She warmed up his clients in a way that he never could.

"Thanks, Ursula. Call me if you need anything."

She waved him off, her scarlet fingers flashing at him before she went back to work. As he made his way through the wide hallway, one of the nearby elevator doors opened with a sharp chime. A woman stepped off looking like she'd just escaped from a hippie colony in the 1960s. Or from Coachella. A crown of bright silk flowers held her thick Afro back from her face while a transparent white blouse—with a convenient horizontal stripe across the chest—cinched into high-waisted jeans shorts that bared an indecent amount of thigh. White gladiator sandals laced up to her knees, and a fringed brown purse completed her look.

Victor greeted his sister without breaking his stride. "Vivian."

"Good boy," she said with a look of relief. "I thought I'd have to take a bite out of your tasty secretary while you dick around in your office." She was the younger by five years, but treated him like a little brother. Victor could admit that at times, she was the stronger of them. When their sister died, she was the one everyone had fallen to for support, while he had just fallen apart. Her flower crowns and thrift store clothes disguised a will of iron.

"I thought you were a vegetarian." He stepped between the elevator doors she held open for him.

"For Ms. Ursula, I'd make an exception."

Vivian chomped her teeth together with a disconcertingly savage sound and grinned at Victor. Apparently that expended too much energy, because she leaned into the elevator wall, thumping the back of her head into the glossy wood. Briefly, she closed her eyes. Then she opened one eye and peered at Victor with all the experience of the entire twenty-seven years she had known him. "You look a little discombobulated, brother. You okay?"

He didn't even try to lie. "Was that guy in *The Godfather* okay when he woke up with the horse head?"

"Is it because of Violet's birthday?" She looked instantly concerned, a frown across her brow. "You know I had a hard time of it, too."

Victor winced now, reminded of his little sister and her death that was never far from his mind. He and Vivian had talked on Violet's birthday, but he'd hung up the phone as soon as he could, preferring to be left alone with his pain. Later that afternoon, he'd met Mella. There was nothing like awaking a previously dormant libido to help distract from emotional hurts.

"I'm listening if you want to talk," Vivian said.

Victor shook his head. "It's not what you think. At least, that's not all of it. But let's wait until we get to the restaurant. I need sustenance for this conversation."

It was less difficult to talk about the sharp ache of missing Violet than his…preoccupation with Mella. But why? It wasn't unusual for him to be attracted to a woman. This wasn't something his sister needed to hear about. But he wasn't being real with himself. He knew exactly what made this situation unusual. He waited until he and Vivian were sitting on the rooftop patio of their favorite Brickell restaurant before he stirred up the wasp's nest that was his sister's curiosity.

At the table, Victor slipped on his sunglasses and almost smiled when Vivian pulled a plastic sun visor from her bag and slipped it over her forehead.

"What?"

He shook his head, lips twisting with amusement. "Why do you always wear these ridiculous things?"

"To make you laugh, of course." She was only half joking. Since his younger sister died nearly fifteen years ago, Victor stopped laughing as much, stopped trying to connect with other people, allowing his natural social unease to become something else.

He took a sip of water to hide the gleam of emotion he knew was in his eyes. Even after all these years and the things they'd been through together, it was still painful for Victor to be so exposed with Vivian. Of the two, he was supposed to be the strong one. The one who made things better and was a rock in the face of life's bullshit. But, better than anyone, he knew that not showing emotion wasn't the same thing as being strong. Vivian was the strong one. He was just coping.

He cleared his throat and tried again for gruff. "When are you going back home?"

Vivian rolled her eyes. "I don't know who you think you're fooling."

His sister lived in Key West, on a tech genius commune with some former college classmates. She was in Miami at least once a month, though, and usually called him with a few hours' notice so he could clear his schedule. He always made time for her. Family meant everything to him.

So although he wanted to keep this thing with Mella to himself—the way it woke things in him he thought long dead—he knew that openness was the currency he paid for keeping her close. It was a currency she exchanged in kind with no hesitation, those pieces of herself that were like gifts to him. But for Victor, that currency came from a bank with limited capital. He rarely felt things deeply. He didn't trust. He hadn't been in a relationship in years. Not since…

"What's weighing on your shoulders so heavily, brother of mine?"

He sighed, getting ready to pay. "There's a woman—"

"Finally!" Vivian cut him off with an excited clap. "It's been forever since you've been with anybody. I tell you, that thing is gonna fall off if you don't use it."

He fixed her with a cool stare. "Do you want to hear the story or not?"

She mimed locking her mouth shut and throwing away the key.

And so, over their lunch, he told her about Michaela Davis and the troubling feelings he had for her, leaving out the more intimate details of his dream life and filling his sister in on the small things she didn't know. How they met. His desire to know more about her, although he knew the impulse was a dangerous one.

"Why is it dangerous? This Mella sounds interesting, and sexy." Vivian grinned across the table at him, looking far more interested than the conversation warranted.

Victor knew very well that in some ways, Mella reminded him of Vivian. Superficially. The way they both seemed to latch on to the beauty in life and ignore the ugliness. The ugliness that was part of his every waking breath.

If he had the financial resources, he imagined that he would be Miami's version of Batman. Taking criminals down one feature-length movie at a time, using his fists to destroy their lives as they'd so carelessly destroyed others. But he wasn't that man. Instead he seethed from his anger. Only letting it out when he stood in the kitchen among steaming pots and pans, or the nights he spent in the gym beating up punching bags and running through his neighborhood as if he could escape his waking dreams.

He was attracted to Mella's sunny spirit like a plant left too long in the shadows. But the last time he'd dared to enjoy a woman beyond his physical desires, it hadn't gone so well. That was two years ago now.

Patrice, who'd been his girlfriend for a little less than a year, hadn't been as radiant as Mella. No one could be. He imagined only the petite woman was blessed with that particularly beguiling and easy smile. Only she was capable of awakening his desire to consume a woman, *that* woman, with his lust until she was trembling and hoarse, sweat-soaked and still begging for him to fill her with his aching love. And then after, he would pull her to him in a bed and press his nose into the damp hollow of her throat and sleep the sleep of the contented, knowing he could wake next to her in the morning and do it all over again.

Victor drew in a surprised breath. That wasn't what he'd meant to say at all.

"She sounds incredible." Vivian was serious now, her brows stitched with worry. Victor shook his head. He wanted to finish the story. If he didn't tell her everything now, it would never come out of him.

"She's beautiful," he said. "And I'm not just talking about her face."

Years ago with Patrice, he thought he'd found happiness with another person. It wasn't a happiness that necessarily made his life easier or even made him feel better about the losses he'd suffered. But it was a thing he could call his own and maybe treasured more than he should have.

He'd met Patrice at one of Kingsley's parties. A gorgeous woman who loved to have fun, she had come to Victor out of nowhere. She charmed him and tried to make him laugh, and before he knew it, she had seduced him out into the club scene that he didn't want to be part of but didn't mind too much since she was at his side.

But she was at his side less and less when they were in those spaces, hanging on to Kingsley's every word, and to other men who shone more brightly than Victor did. He watched her with a steadily building sense of dread, even as she pressed him to "lighten up" and "try to relax." And he even tried that for her sake, but eventually thought those things were beyond him. His pleasures were simple, but they were keen and they were his. Still, he'd fooled himself into thinking she was satisfied with how things were until he walked in on her trying to seduce Kingsley.

The night was etched in his mind. Another one of Kingsley's wild parties. Women, liquor and movie stars in every corner of the Bal Harbour penthouse. A different type of music set the mood in every room Victor walked into, lending a kind of schizophrenic air to his meanderings. He nursed his habitual ginger ale and tried to enjoy himself for Patrice's sake.

He ended up talking politics and practicing his Arabic with a visiting diplomat from Eritrea. As they talked, the man became less diplomatic, and instead began to badger Victor about America's belligerent foreign policy and general lack of diplomacy. The topics were nothing Victor was invested in, but it felt good to have a lively conversation and speak a language he rarely had any opportunity to.

When the ambassador excused himself to talk to his wife on the phone, Victor moved on to find Kingsley. At the door to his friend's study, he heard Patrice's soft voice, but there was something else in it, a touch of the intimacy she used when trying to get him to do something he was reluctant to.

Victor didn't sneak. He had no reason to. The rug quieted his footsteps, and it didn't take him long to be at the open door and watch with quiet horror as Patrice slinked toward Kingsley, who stood with his arms crossed and a drink in his hand.

"He doesn't understand me like you do, King," she said with that seductive tremor in her voice.

But Kingsley didn't seem seduced. "That's something you should discuss with Victor, not me."

"He wouldn't get it." Patrice was only a few inches from Kingsley, her white dress backless and clinging to every curve. Victor felt frozen to the floor.

With a snakelike movement, Patrice tugged down the top of her dress, baring her breasts and flat stomach to Kingsley. "But you can get it."

A flash of some emotion crossed Kingsley's face, but he didn't move. Finally, he gestured to Patrice's bare chest. "Get dressed. It's time for you to leave."

Patrice gave a breathless laugh, seduction still on ten. "But don't you want a taste of this, King? You know everyone else does."

Victor couldn't see what she did with her hand and

her bare chest. All he saw was the look on Kingsley's face. Disappointment. Anger. Revulsion.

Kingsley didn't address Patrice's invitation. "I want you to leave this house and don't come back. And…" Here Kingsley paused. "Don't see Victor again. You don't deserve to clean his shit-stained boots with your tongue." He said it matter-of-factly, as if he was commenting on the temperature of the ice in his glass.

Patrice's head jerked back and her hands flew to her naked chest, fumbling to yank the dress back up. She drew in a loud breath in preparation to speak. It was then that Victor unfroze and walked fully into the room, making sure to walk heavily so they both heard him.

Kingsley put aside his glass and turned away from Patrice while she finished dealing with her dress, words already tumbling from her mouth.

"I was just looking for you, Victor." She smoothed down the back of her dress.

"You should go," he said, keeping his voice deliberately mild. He wanted to shout at her, demand what she was doing with him if Kingsley was who she really wanted.

"It's not what you think," Patrice said, running her fingers through the long sweep of hair over her shoulder. "I was just asking—"

Victor cut her off before she could lie to him anymore. "I'm not thinking at all now actually." He sat in an armchair and took the fresh glass of ginger ale on ice that Kingsley automatically offered him. "Maybe I haven't been thinking the entire time we've been together." Only a year, but that was significant for him. "Please." He never pleaded with anyone. "Just go."

Unbelievably, she snapped at him. "This is King's house, not yours."

"You heard what the man said," Kingsley growled from near the window. "He didn't stutter, and neither did I."

She stared at them both, openmouthed for a moment before she turned in a clatter of high heels and nearly ran from the study. Victor remembered feeling the breath leave his chest in a rush, closing his eyes tight so he wouldn't see his friend's look of sympathy.

He'd been working so hard at trying to love Patrice that he confused the abrupt release of the tight feeling in his chest, the tingling in his palms, for something other than the relief it was. He was glad Kingsley was the one Patrice had tried it with. Any other man, and all of Miami would know she was using him, simply climbing toward the next rich man on her back.

"Sorry about that," Kingsley said after she was gone. "I didn't know she was that kind." He topped up Victor's ginger ale and clinked their glasses to the relief of near misses.

But Victor hadn't been able to dismiss it so easily. Two years later, the experience still twisted inside him like a blade broken off in a long-ago wound. He hadn't been with a woman since.

"You can't let one trashy bitch spoil it for everyone else, Victor." Vivian pointed her salad-laden fork at him. "This new girl doesn't seem anything like Patrice."

He shrugged. Vivian didn't know. Then again, neither did he. Mella could be perfect. She could also be Aileen Wuornos reincarnated. It was a toss-up. But none of that mattered. He didn't want to trust Michaela Davis. He didn't want to want her. Although from the kiss they'd shared in his office—and a heaviness settled low in his stomach as he remembered how she tasted—*want* didn't seem like a strong enough word for the burning she stirred in him.

Victor shifted in his seat. But even this, he knew, was only a basic physical response and would disappear as soon as he got his thoughts under control. He didn't *need* to satisfy that desire for her. Celibacy was no problem for him.

"You're such a chatterbox sometimes, brother dear. I never get a word in edgewise." Vivian teased him with a light tap on his wrist after he'd been quiet for too long.

He roused himself enough to tease his sister in return. "I was actually thinking about how hard she made me from just one kiss."

Vivian scrunched up her face. "You could have actually kept that to yourself."

"I thought you wanted to hear everything." He challenged her with a raised eyebrow, a smile curling his mouth.

"Too much, Vic. Too much."

"You know, she—" He almost told her that Kingsley was the one Mella seemed to fit better with. But saying that seemed ridiculous in the face of everything he'd just said. He just needed to hash this out with his best friend and cut his losses before they added up to a broken friendship. So he sipped his ginger ale instead. "None of that is really important. Tell me, what are you up to these days?"

A brief frown appeared on Vivian's face, the beginnings of her pushing the subject. Then she made an airy motion, reading him like a cheap paperback. "I thought you'd never ask…"

After lunch with Vivian, Victor felt too keyed up by their conversation to focus completely on work. Instead of taking one of his current projects home with him or even going to the gym, he finished up in the office a little after six and went to one of his favorite places in the city.

Gillespie's was a lounge and restaurant he went to on a semiregular basis, often enough that the people there knew him, including its celebrity owner, a model and entrepreneur he often saw on billboards around the city. Victor's comfort, bred by years of familiarity, was ensured at the large restaurant and bar. He returned a nod from the doorman and the knowing glance of one of the servers who regularly took care of his favorite spot in the bar, a quiet and mostly hidden corner with a table for one.

Being alone at home would've made more sense, but on this evening of all evenings, he wanted the chaos of strangers around him. He wanted the comfortable anonymity that Gillespie's could provide.

Instead of heading to his favorite table, he slid onto the smooth leather of one of the bar stools, a sigh easing from his throat. The bartender nodded at him, and he nodded back at her, then raised his glass in thanks when she slid a ginger ale on ice in front of him only moments later. He let the nearby conversations roll over him, allowing his mind to wander, knowing no one would bother him.

The guy two stools down from him was drinking some kind of whiskey, something bottom shelf by the smell of it. Victor swirled the ginger ale in his glass and watched the bubbling golden waves dip and sway over the ice. He sipped. Although he didn't mind alcohol, could watch it being poured, even stand the smell of it up close, the thought of drinking it made his throat clutch with nausea, made him remember the night of his sister's death and all the drinks he'd had while she bled out in the street. The drinks that hadn't stopped him from getting behind the wheel just like the stupid drunk driver who'd killed her. He swallowed hard and deliberately turned his thoughts away from Violet.

The other things he had to think about were unpleasant enough.

A rumble of unease vibrated in his throat. He wanted Mella with a strength that was terrifying. But he loved Kingsley like a brother. He was sure he and his best friend had had their share of fights over the years, but he couldn't remember what about. The two of them had been friends since before they could properly write their names, strange boys in the same kindergarten class who happened to both like Jet Li and *Gargoyles*, the cartoon. Other than that, they'd rarely gravitated toward similar things.

Kingsley was outgoing and loved to party and date

as many women as he could feasibly entertain, although he didn't sleep with nearly as many as people assumed. Victor liked cooking, relaxing at home, taking the occasional rented boat up north in winter.

Now, as adults, the two met in the middle at a mutual love of chess, the Investigation Discovery channel, inside jokes and German chocolate cake. Kingsley was Victor's friend, and no matter how much he liked Mella, he would give up the chance to make love to her just because his friend wanted her.

Victor took a sip of ginger ale, crunched an ice cube between his teeth and idly watched the basketball game on mute behind the bar. There was no second-guessing it. He would let his attraction to her go, but he had to confess to Kingsley first that he had broken their unspoken rule of never getting mixed up with the same women. Air hissed from between his teeth.

Down the bar from him, a pair of women, dressed alike but obviously not sisters, giggled over their pink martinis and kept glancing toward a group of men nearby. Victor was peripherally aware of their giggling for what seemed like a damn long time before finally, one of the men they were chittering about approached, smiling broadly with a wave of his hand to indicate both women. It took Victor a moment to recognize Carter Diallo, one of Kingsley's younger brothers. Not far away was a gathering of Diallo men, at least all the single ones. They looked big and hungry, a pack of alpha males on the hunt for fresh meat. Victor smiled grimly at the analogy. That had never been a sport that appealed to him, the hunting for nightly companionship, even before Patrice had gotten her claws into him.

When Victor paid better attention, he saw that there were other women nearby, some of them obviously paired off with the brothers. But the two giggling women, despite being brought over by Carter, seemed totally focused on one man. And that man was Kingsley. Victor did a double take when he saw how Kingsley responded to the giggling women. He swept an arm around them and pulled them to him, grinning as if he'd caught the ultimate prize of the night.

Victor stiffened. What was Kingsley doing hunting when he could be wooing Mella? He bristled with jealousy on her behalf, teeth crunching into another piece of ice as he watched Kingsley with the women. What could his friend see in them when he already had Mella, a diamond compared to these pebbles on the beach? He put his nearly empty glass on the bar, slid a bill underneath it and waded into the pack of Diallo men.

They all greeted him with handshakes and loose smiles that spoke to how long they'd been at the bar.

"Vic, what are you doing here on a school night?" Kingsley moved away from the women to squeeze Victor's shoulder.

"Bum-rushing a meeting in the boys' room, apparently."

"Nothing that high school. We're celebrating Lex's promotion." He playfully grabbed his brother's elbow, although Lex was already talking to a woman in bright blue stilettos. Lex shrugged off Kingsley's hold after a vague nod in Victor's direction and went back to more important things. Alexander, one of the few grown Diallo children who didn't have a position at the family's multibillion-dollar corporation, was something of a rebel. He did his own thing, always had, and apparently was content to continue doing so.

"Congratulations," Victor said to Lex once the girl wandered off to the bar for a drink.

"Thanks!" Lex indicated a mostly empty table nearby. "You should join us if you're feeling like company."

"Thanks for the offer, but I'm about to leave," Victor said. "Enjoy the action, though."

"You know I will." Lex stalked off after the girl.

Victor jerked his head at Kingsley. "Talk to you for a sec?"

"Yeah, sure." They stepped away from the group and moved without discussion to the bar where Victor had been drinking by himself.

Once they were alone, or as alone as they could be in a bar with dozens of other patrons on a weeknight, Victor gripped Kingsley's arm. "What the hell are you doing?"

Kingsley looked down, frowning, at the fingers curled in the thin material of his shirt. "Having a good time. The usual. What's up with you right now?" He shrugged off Victor's grip.

"What about M—" He bit off the sound of Mella's name, wincing at the intimate feel of it just on his tongue. His attraction to her was already so far out of hand. "What about Mella? She'd probably appreciate you giving the other women a break for a while."

"What does your girl have to do with me?"

"My girl?"

Kingsley gave Victor a look that said he seriously doubted his intelligence. "Yeah. The girl you've been losing your mind over since the second you saw her."

"What are you talking about?" His mind was firmly intact, dammit. "You and she were all chummy at the auction and at the game. You even have the same—" he searched for the phrase "—butterfly theory of relationships."

"Please." Kingsley looked offended. "When have I ever—" He broke off. "Wait a minute. You thought she and I—" He laughed now, the corners of his pale brown eyes crinkling with humor. "She's not my type. I like girls who actually like me. You know that."

Victor did know that. But it was a rare woman—did she even exist?—who didn't like Kingsley. Mella had certainly responded to his jokes and ready laughter. Watching her with him was the first time Victor remembered ever being jealous of his friend.

"So you don't want her?" he asked.

"Hell no!"

Victor's eyes narrowed.

"Not that she's a dog or anything!" Kingsley held up his hands in defense, as if Victor was about to punch him in the face. Maybe Victor even wanted to, a little. "She's sexy as hell." Victor frowned again, and Kingsley backed away, laughing. "No disrespect, but I'm not the one she's always asking about and giving sex eyes to."

"Sex eyes?" Victor was only peripherally aware of

his body weakening with relief. Kingsley wasn't interested in Mella. Mella wasn't interested in Kingsley.

"Yeah, you know what I'm talking about. She looks like she's imagining you in her bed, all spread out with some chocolate sauce and whipped—"

"Okay, that's enough!"

Kingsley chuckled. "Good!" He draped an arm around Victor's shoulder. "I wasn't sure how much longer I could go on talking about her and your junk." He turned them toward the bar. "Now, let me buy you a celebratory drink. I assume you're going after her now, right? Make that whipped-cream fantasy of hers come true."

Victor winced through his smile of relief. "You can really stop now, at any time."

A belly laugh vibrated his friend's solid frame. "A San Pellegrino with lime, then, on me. Let's live a little tonight." Kingsley signaled the bartender while Victor grinned at his friend's foolishness.

Two stools down, Mr. Cheap Whiskey ordered another drink, still looking as tightly wound as Victor felt half an hour before. From long ago experience, he knew solutions never lay at the bottom of a bottle. But sometimes a bitter sort of respite waited there. Victor thought again of his sister, her accident and the night he could never forget. When the bartender made her way to him with his mineral water and a vodka tonic for Kingsley, he slid her enough money to pay the stranger's tab. Kingsley glanced briefly at him, then nodded in understanding.

They raised their glasses to each other in a silent toast. *To friendship and all its blessings.*

Chapter 5

Aunt Jess's favorite biker bar had the best chicken wings in Miami. Mella reached for a flat already dipped in blue-cheese dressing, while her aunt scooped up a loaded nacho. They both sighed around their delicious mouthfuls of food. Of all the things Mella had in common with her aunt, she was the most grateful that they loved food with an equal passion.

"These are *so* good." She spoke around a bite of the barbecue-and-blue-cheese-flavored meat. "Sometimes you make me wish I was a biker so I could just come here by myself and eat all the wings."

Her aunt chuckled weakly, trying to put on a brave face despite what Mella knew was on her mind. "You don't have to be a biker to eat here, Michaela."

"Yeah, but they look at me like they know I'm not

and don't approve." Although maybe she could pull out her vintage leather jacket and boots to fool them with her best bad-girl swagger.

"You're in your head again." Another smile from her aunt.

"Aren't I always?"

At lunchtime, the bar in the Black Grove was crowded with a noisy and raucous horde that laughed and chatted with an unbridled energy and enthusiasm Mella never saw in fancier restaurants. Mella knew her aunt found it comforting, these people who were like the parents Jess grew up with, although she was brought up in private schools and generally sheltered in the lap of luxury that her parents' lottery win and smart investing had brought.

Mella loved that her aunt never tried to be anyone other than who she was. She enjoyed the luxuries her parents' money had brought, but she never made a secret of preferring their way, being with people who said what they meant instead of using excuses of "gentility" to stab each other in the back.

Her aunt loved this life, but had kept it for herself, not wanting her son to be exposed to its comforting roughness. A roughness that could have saved him from diving headfirst into the dangerous trust-fund kids' lifestyle that had ended with him in jail.

Which was what brought them to Rooster's Bar and Grill in the middle of the day. Shaun's parole hearing was coming up soon. Aunt Jess was worried about the outcome but didn't want to talk outright about it. Mella was willing to dance with her around the subject that had the corners of her eyes tight despite her smile.

A young man walked past them, small but aggressive looking in his studded leather jacket and boots. There was a stink on him, a certain vulnerability in the way he walked, the bulge of the oversize pack on his back that reminded Mella of the homeless kids she and Nala were trying to help. Her aunt must have seen it, too.

"How is the work on Sanctuary coming along?" she asked.

Mella pulled her gaze from the boy. "It's going great," she said. "The plans have already been drawn up, and work on the grounds started earlier this week." The day before, she and Nala had dropped by to take a look at the work in progress. Already, there were significant changes to the weed-choked grounds of the mansion. "Victor says it shouldn't take more than a couple of months."

"*Victor*, huh?" Her aunt caught on to something in her voice right away. Or was it in the way she licked her lips when Victor's name brushed across them?

"Yes, he's the landscape architect working on the project. He's very impressive."

"Him or his work?"

"Both?" It didn't take much for Mella to remember that afternoon in his office—the unexpected kiss they'd shared that had gone from hot to incendiary between one heartbeat and the next. His hands steadying her hips. The press of his hard body against hers that could have easily led to her being spread across his desk and screwed breathless.

But the physical was something she understood. It

was the literal electric connection between them that made her worry. That and the way his dark eyes explored her face as if there was something in her he was searching for. Something she wasn't quite sure existed, but wanted to be there. Just for him.

"Guh!" She put down the bones of the latest decimated chicken wing and took a long sip of her peach iced tea.

Aunt Jess laughed. "Is he the reason you were so distracted the other day?"

Mella could never lie to her aunt. "Yes." She took a breath, not quite knowing what to say about Victor. She was drawn to him. He had kissed her. They were stuck together for the remainder of the Sanctuary project. But did any of that mean anything?

"He's very solemn. He doesn't laugh, but there's something about him I can't ignore." She shrugged, feeling like she was babbling. "I don't know."

Her aunt nudged the last of the wings on the wide plate toward Mella and snagged the remaining sweet potato fries for herself. "You don't know what to do with a serious man who knows what he wants," she said.

"Maybe I don't. But should I want anything from him? He's not like anybody I've ever dated. I don't want anything serious, and he just seems like that type. You know I prefer—" she searched for the right word "—butterfly interludes to anything society tells us that we should want."

"Sometimes I think you're just being contrary, saying no to monogamy and potential happily-ever-after because that's what most people you know want or have." Aunt Jess waved a fry at her. "There's nothing wrong with being happy with one person, Michaela."

"You know that's not why being coupled is not my thing." She held a piece of chicken in front of her face but did not bite into it. "It's more complicated than that."

"I know, honey." They exchanged a glance filled with the pain of the past that always managed to spill over into their present lives. "But not everybody leaves." Aunt Jess waved a dismissive hand. "Besides, you don't know what this man wants. Have you talked about it with him?"

"No." The tightness in Mella's chest loosened. No, she didn't want to talk about what had formed her relationship habits. That was a discussion for the fifth of never. "We haven't had many conversations that weren't about work. It seems like the safest thing."

"When have you ever done the safe thing?" Another French fry disappeared into her aunt's mouth.

Mella made a growling noise. "Don't dare me to go there, Aunt Jess."

"I'm not daring you. If you want this man, take him. You know how short life is."

They both fell into thoughtful silence, the river of the past eddying between them. Mella's parents. They had died crossing the street on their way to get ice cream cones, for God's sake. Mella bit her lip, trying to push the familiar sadness away. Her parents were gone, their deaths the reason she couldn't see any point in committing to anyone. Life would just take away everything she had and leave nothing but pain behind. It was a stupid way to live. Her aunt cautioned her about that time and time again. But if it ain't broke, don't fix it. Right?

Mella took another big sip of her iced tea, needing the liquid to soothe the heat from the spicy barbecue.

"I'm going to the hearing," her aunt said suddenly. "The parole hearing."

Mella put down her glass. "Do you want me to come with you?"

"No, no. I don't want to…" Her voice trailed off.

Mella read behind her aunt's hesitation. Aunt Jess was scared the hearing might not go her way. She didn't want Mella to see her cry when she was denied her son.

Over the years Shaun had been away, he seemed to have genuinely changed from the brash, entitled boy he was at nineteen. He'd written letters of apology to the victim's family, swore he would never drink another drop of alcohol, even begged Aunt Jess's forgiveness for putting her through all the years of worry and pain. But Mella knew these things were no guarantee that the parole board would rule in his favor.

"It's okay," Mella said. "I'll keep that day free in case you change your mind. But you know I'm only a phone call away, no matter what happens."

Her aunt somehow found a real smile and reached across the table with her sticky hand. "I know, sweet girl."

"Ew!" Mella playfully swatted away her aunt's sauce-stained hand. "The least you can do is use that hand to order us some more chicken," she said. "That platter wasn't enough." She looked down at the debris of bones and sauce on the plate between them.

"Since you asked me so nicely." Her aunt signaled a passing waitress.

Mella didn't really want any more wings. Already she would have to do extra in the gym tonight. But it was worth it to distract her aunt from her obviously dour thoughts. She patted her stomach with a sigh. The sacrifices she had to make…

The late-morning sun was warm. Almost too warm, lightly roasting Mella's shoulders even with the sunscreen she'd managed to smear on at the last minute. She and Liz were taking a day to themselves to wander through as many Sunday-morning markets around Miami as possible. This was their third. Mangoes and a few nectarines weighed down the backpack on Mella's shoulder. Liz only had a half dozen avocados in her plastic bag.

Wearing shorts and a belly-baring tank top, her friend sipped from her plastic cup of freshly squeezed fruit juice from the organic juice man. But she kept sneaking glances at Mella's goat-cheese-and-turkey-sausage crepe while chewing on her straw. Mella rolled her eyes at her friend and nibbled on the pieces of Swiss chard poking out from the sides of her crepe.

Liz liked to eat almost as much as Mella did, but was always starving herself for one foolish reason or another. Well, it was actually only for one reason: to find the husband of her dreams.

"No man wants a fat chick, Mella," Liz said as if reading Mella's thoughts.

Mella licked smears of goat cheese from the corners of her mouth. "No man wants skin and bones, Liz. I don't know where you get the idea you have to be a bag of sticks to find a husband." Her friend was worrying far too much about her weight.

"But I can't eat all the stuff I want *and* find somebody to marry me." Liz chewed viciously on her straw, looking even more resentful that she didn't get a crepe for herself.

"Then just exercise and keep eating what you want. You're not even thick, Liz. You should probably eat more. From what I see in music videos, girls with fat booties are what men want." Mella gave a dirty laugh, knowing that Liz hated "video hoes" with a passion. Sometimes Mella thought it was only because she secretly wanted to be one.

Liz gave her a narrow-eyed look. "Easy for you to say when you weigh next to nothing."

"That's because I'm always kickboxing or running my life away on the treadmill at home. Just because you don't see me eating salads for every meal doesn't mean I'm not doing something to burn off all the chicken wings and cheese-covered apple pies I love." She chewed a bite of crepe that was mostly goat cheese. "I like my food, and I'm not going to stop eating just so I can impress some man who probably doesn't care how much I weigh, anyway."

"Easy for you to say when you have a million guys chasing after you."

Mella snorted at her friend's exaggeration. A few guys turned on by a woman who owned her own business definitely didn't amount to a million. "A million, huh? Was that the stampeding sound I heard?"

"Whatever. You never even try, and you have guys practically promising you all the diamonds on Saturn." They'd just watched a documentary explaining that it rained diamonds on Saturn and Jupiter.

It was probably Liz's air of matrimonial desperation that turned men off, Mella thought. If she were a man, she'd be put off in the fine art of skirt chasing, too, if the prey practically lay down in front of her with the leash in their teeth.

"Just chill with the husband hunting, Lizzy. What you want will come to you." She purposely sidestepped any mention of Victor or any other man supposedly chasing her.

Liz slurped the last of the juice from her cup as they neared the lot where Mella had parked. They waited on the sidewalk for a dark SUV to pull in from the street in front of them.

"Hey, that's—"

But Mella had already seen him. Victor Raphael with sunglasses on, driving his big Mercedes truck with one hand. He pulled smoothly into the parking lot and came to a stop not far from where they stood. Mella finished the last bite of her crepe and wiped her mouth with a napkin. "Yes, that is him." Without saying anything else, she kept walking.

"Mella and Victor sitting in a tree…" Liz sang softly at her side.

"If you don't stop, I'm going to trip you," Mella said through clenched teeth.

Liz giggled. "You wouldn't." But she stopped singing, anyway. They both knew she was too cute to fall in public. As they drew closer to the Mercedes, Mella paused. Should she stop and say hello to Victor? The decision spilled out of her hands when the doors of the SUV opened and Victor climbed out. He saw her right away.

"Mella." He shut his door just as the other doors opened. A young and barely dressed woman clambered out of the passenger side and latched on to Victor's arm.

"Are you going to introduce us?" The woman looked briefly at Victor, who stared at Mella with an unreadable expression. Was this his girlfriend? Someone he'd spent the night with? The thought twisted the knife of jealousy in Mella's belly.

The woman was tall like Victor, and humor made beauty of what could have easily been an unremarkable face. A white lace ribbon wove through the high crown of her Afro, and she wore a short white dress, loose and lacy, with ankle-high gladiator sandals. She looked like a fairy queen. Compared to her, Mella felt very unimpressive in her T-shirt and tight jeans.

The back doors of the truck opened, distracting Mella from the woman who was possibly dating Victor. Another woman appeared, this one stunningly beautiful and older, wearing jeans and a T-shirt that told everyone to Save the Everglades.

"That was good driving," the older woman was saying to someone still in the truck. "You can learn a thing or two from your son."

"I drive just fine," a male voice grumbled from inside the truck. Then a tall, distinguished man joined the other woman, blinking into the hot sun before the woman pulled a pair of sunglasses from her purse and shoved them at him. He put on the glasses without hesitation. It was obvious now that they were married.

"I'm not in a rush," the older man said.

Mella noticed immediately the features he had in common with Victor—the skin like new pennies and an upright bearing that made him seem even taller than his six-plus feet. But he had freckles scattered across his nose and cheeks…freckles that looked very much like those on the younger woman's face.

Oh…

She wiped her mouth, just in case there were any lingering smears of goat cheese, and smiled gamely at Victor and his family. "Hey." She smiled at the girl who stood at Victor's side, certain now that she was his sister.

"I'm Vivian. Victor's my brother. He got his good looks from me." She reached up to pinch Victor's cheeks and winked at Mella.

She surprised a laugh out of Mella, who was so relieved Vivian wasn't his girlfriend that she spontaneously reached past the other woman's handshake for a hug. "You were very generous with your gift, thank you."

If she hadn't been watching him closely, Mella would have missed the faintest touch of a smile to Victor's mouth. But she *had* been watching. She also noticed there was something different in how he looked at her. The last time, despite their kiss that had her begging for more of his touch, he'd held back from her. But today, he was all in, his stare open and devouring, dark eyes lit from within as if he could look into the very heart of her and strip away her pretenses, her *clothes*, to see and incite every bit of desire she had for him.

"Wait a minute now," Victor's father said and broke her not-so-subtle stare at his son. "If anyone, he got those looks from me." He came closer with a teasing smile, reflecting Mella in the twin mirrors of his sunglasses. She reflexively checked her teeth for Swiss chard in the mirrors, then shrugged when he caught her, laughing at her own foolishness. "I'm Mella," she said. "I'm working on a project with Victor." She reached back to grab Liz's hand. "And this is my friend Liz."

"Hey." Liz waved with her empty juice cup, barely hiding a smirk at Mella's expense. Here in the flesh was one of the so-called "million" guys Mella didn't acknowledge.

"We were just heading over to get some fresh juice." Vivian pointed at Liz's cup. "Does the juice man still have stuff left to make it?"

"He's got more than enough," Liz said. "I ordered a large with everything in it, but he still had plenty more fruit and sugar cane after he made mine."

"Good." Victor's mother pulled another pair of sunglasses from her bag and slid them on with an impatient sigh.

"Never mind Mama," Vivian said. "She has no manners when she's hungry."

But if Victor's mother was dismissive, his father was the opposite.

"It's good to meet you," he said, extending two hands to warmly clasp Mella's. He glanced at Victor, then back to her. "I've heard some interesting things about you."

Victor jumped in with a warning frown. "Dad—"

"Excuse my father." Vivian grabbed her father's hand and pulled him away from Mella. "He's weird all the time."

Mella felt she was missing something. But she mentally shrugged. "That's okay. Weird is good."

Behind Vivian, Victor's mother made impatient motions. Mella could take a hint.

"It was great seeing you all." She waved them off before Victor's mother could keel over from low blood sugar. "I'll see you soon," she said to Victor, then pulled Liz away. Although she didn't watch them leave, she felt Victor's eyes on her, an intimate caress that made her aware of the sway of her hips, the tight fit of her jeans around her thighs. She handed Liz a helmet and the backpack with their morning's spoils.

"We have one more market on our list, then we can quit," Mella said, although she wasn't really feeling it anymore.

"This hot-ass sun wore me out." Liz jammed the helmet on her head and shrugged into the leather jacket Mella pulled from the motorcycle's saddlebag. "Let's find something else to do."

Mella was relieved they were on the same page. "Corinne's at that pool party in Fort Lauderdale. We should crash that." Mella got on the motorcycle, and Liz mounted up behind her.

"I hope they have booze." Liz dropped down the visor of her helmet and grabbed onto Mella's waist.

"Corinne always has booze," Mella called out over the rumble of the bike's engine. "That's why we like her so much."

Her friend laughed, and Mella slowly navigated the bike through the busy parking lot and out into the street. From the corner of her eye, she thought she saw Victor watching her ride away, but it might have just been her imagination. And wishful thinking.

"Enjoy your chai, Ms. Taylor." Mella handed her regular customer a handful of change and a receipt. "See you again tomorrow."

The woman waved and stepped back to wait for her drink, and Mella turned to the next customer with a greeting on the tip of her tongue, but when she saw who it was, her mouth snapped shut. Victor stood in front of the register.

She felt inexplicably glad, a thread of happiness winding through her at the sight of him, so serious and compelling, his grim face and clothes at odds with the buzzing cheerfulness of the café. In addition to his usual black shirt, slacks and blazer, this time there was a tie involved, also black, that made him look like he was coming back from a funeral. Or a murder.

A spontaneous smile curved her lips. "Victor, how nice to see you."

Kingsley leaned in her direction with a soft laugh, deliberately bringing attention to himself. "Good afternoon, Ms. Davis."

Mella fought the blush that climbed into her face. God! Why was she being so damn obvious? "Good afternoon, Kingsley. Good to see you, too."

"Not as good as seeing Victor, I'm sure. But just so you know, I'm the one who brought him here." He shouldered his friend aside with a fond smile. "Do I at least get some free points on my frequent customer card for that?"

Victor bumped Kingsley's shoulder in retaliation, the slightest of frowns on his face. "The only thing you'll get for free is oxygen so you can order something like a normal person."

Mella gaped. Did Victor just tell a joke?

Kingsley laughed. He ordered a black coffee, two croissants and a kale salad. "And I'll pay for whatever Victor's having."

Victor ordered a black coffee for himself. "You make that apron look good," he said in lieu of an actual "hello." Was this him flirting? Mella grinned, finally getting into the spirit.

"Thank you." She batted her eyes at him. "You make funereal look sexy. Because of you, the all-black look is making a comeback."

"It never left," Kingsley said as he dumped the entire change from the fifty he'd given her into the tip jar.

Mella honest-to-God giggled. "Your order will be

waiting for you over there." She tipped her head toward the counter nearby and watched the two men walk away to the stares of most of the female customers in the café.

It was a good thing she was a decent multitasker because she was able to ring up other customers, make correct change and keep her eye on Victor at the same time. He and Kingsley took a seat by the front window. Odd, since most people chose to sit at one of the sidewalk tables where they could catch a glimpse of the water and the bathing suit–clad pedestrians.

"I think you gave me too much change, miss." A young girl gave Mella a puzzled look and held out what was obviously change for twenty dollars in her hand, when she'd only given Mella five dollars for her iced coffee.

Mella blushed. "Sorry, honey."

"It's okay," the girl said. "I can't keep my eyes off them, either." She grinned and stepped toward the pickup counter after she got her correct change. Maybe Mella wasn't as good at multitasking as she thought.

When Colin, her lunch backup, came to relieve her, she gratefully accepted his offer to take over the register. On a normal day she'd have told him to relax and let her handle the rest of the line already waiting. But with Victor in the café, she could barely remember her own name.

"Thanks, Colin."

The boy smiled at her and slid a look in the corner of the café to where Victor and Kingsley sat. "You're welcome, Mella." He neatly put on his apron while she made change for the latest customer. "Why don't you sit down and I'll bring you a cup of tea? You look a little *thirsty*." He jerked his pointy chin toward the men.

Mella only just stopped herself from sticking her tongue out at him.

But she did leave to wash her hands in the employee bathroom and make herself presentable before approaching their table, hot tea in hand. "May I join you?"

Both men immediately got to their feet, though Victor was the one who looked her over from head to toe in a quick, devouring glance.

"We'd be disappointed if you didn't," Kingsley said.

Victor grabbed a chair from a nearby empty table for her. She sat with a grateful smile. "Thank you."

His response was a flicker of eyelashes, a light finger on her bare shoulder before going back to his own seat. She shivered beneath his far-from-casual touch.

Thankfully, Kingsley didn't seem to notice a thing. "This is a great place, Mella." He glanced around the café with a pleased smile. "My sister, Alice, comes here a lot, or at least the location close to our parents' house on Key Biscayne. We don't know if she's become a caffeine addict or if there's a boy she's obsessed with."

"We do have a lot of cute guys working at that location."

"Have you dated any of them?" This was the first time Victor said something while Mella was at the table. She and Kingsley both stared at him.

Kingsley's look was one of pure amusement. He leaned back, apparently content to wait and see what Mella had to say.

"I don't believe in interoffice dating," she said after sipping carefully from the mug of hot tea.

"A good policy," Kingsley said. "Crapping where you eat is generally not a good idea."

"I think as long as you use the designated toilets, that's fine." Victor's words brought Mella's gaze back to his face. "So, back to my exact question—have you ever dated any of your coworkers?"

"Why do you want to know? Curiosity, or do you want to date me yourself?"

Kingsley didn't hide his laughter. "You walked straight into that one, Vic."

Mella wrinkled her nose at the nickname but didn't back down from Victor's stare. Just then, one of the girls from behind the counter, Roshelle, brought a small plate for the table. "Your kale salad, sir."

Mella automatically looked at the food, making sure it was well presented and appeared appetizing. With slivers of almonds, glistening pieces of kale and brilliantly red cranberries, the salad was beautiful. Kingsley apparently thought the same because he made a sound of appreciation before picking up his fork.

"Mmm. This is really good," he said.

Mella grinned with pride. "I'm glad you enjoy it."

"It's not better than the one Victor makes, though." Kingsley nudged the plate toward his friend. "Try it."

Victor shook his head. "I'll take your word for it." He took a sip from his black coffee and seemed to move even farther back from the plate.

But Kingsley didn't seem bothered. "If you ate his kale salad or anything else he makes, you'll find yourself praising gods you never knew existed." He forked in another mouthful, humming his pleasure.

"He eats anything you put in front of him," Victor said to Mella.

"Not true." Kingsley waved a fork at his friend. "Remember when you made that pureed octopus stew?" They both looked slightly nauseated for a moment before Kingsley took a quick sip of his coffee, a palate cleanser apparently, before digging back into the salad.

"Yes," Victor said thoughtfully. "Certain things should be left unexplored. And it was a waste of a perfectly good octopus." He, too, sipped his coffee, a faint frown between his brows.

"The only thing with tentacles I've ever had is calamari," Mella said. She thought with a flare of sudden hunger of one of her favorite dishes and the best place in town to get it. Did she have enough time to get an order to go from Gillespie's? "I *love* calamari."

"Everyone likes calamari," Victor said.

Then Kingsley chimed in. "Everyone likes *fried things*."

"True," Mella agreed. She hated okra on principle; the grossness factor of dealing with the slime wasn't worth any supposed nutritional content of the vegetable…or was it a fruit? But she had tried fried okra before on a dare from her aunt and loved it.

"You should invite her over for dinner, Victor," Kingsley said, plucking a large piece of kale out of the bowl. "Maybe this weekend?"

Mella had the feeling that the surprised look on Victor's face only mirrored her own. Kingsley glanced up, catching Mella's eye with a wink before turning to Victor. "You can try out the tagine recipe you were talking about last week." He turned to Mella. "He's a decent landscape architect but a damn excellent chef."

"Cook." Victor's correction sounded both automatic and often-made. "Chefs have degrees, or at least a restaurant to run. I have neither."

"Fine. Victor here is a master cook. You haven't experienced a real meal until you sit down at his table and eat what he feeds you."

Mella was intrigued. Although, like Kingsley, she generally ate anything put in front of her, she rarely met a chef—or cook—who actually impressed her. She loved certain foods, but when something was good, like the wings at Rooster's or the banana milkshake at Steak 'n Shake, she was hooked for life. "Is this invitation from you, too? I wouldn't want to come anywhere I'm not invited."

"Yes," Victor said, looking a bit shell-shocked. "Of course you're welcome to come over and have a meal at my house. Anytime."

Kingsley sat back with his empty salad bowl and a look of satisfaction on his handsome face. "Would it be too much if I ordered seconds?"

As Kingsley pondered one of the great questions of the universe, Mella noticed a familiar pair of boys walking into the café. The boys were nearly identical in their thinness. They wore tight jeans that had seen better days and T-shirts stretched across their skinny chests. They could have been twins, but she knew from one unforgettable conversation that the two boys were lovers.

Kelvin and DeAndre.

Mella stood up, brushing Victor's shoulder as she passed. "Excuse me a second." She felt rather than saw his look of surprise that she'd touched him, and then she put him at the back of her mind for the moment. Mella reached the counter before the boys did.

"Hey, guys. It's good to see you again. It's been a while."

Kelvin and DeAndre looked at her like they always did, as if they were surprised she recognized them, although they'd been coming into the café on and off for nearly two months now. Like most days, it was DeAndre who spoke.

"Hi, Ms. Davis." She allowed the "Ms. Davis" to slide since she was probably at least fifteen years older than them. DeAndre shoved his hand in his pocket, digging deep to bring up a pair of crumpled dollar bills and some change. "A large cup of coffee, please."

"Of course." She offered them her warmest smile, glad to see them.

It had to be hard for such delicate-looking boys to live on the streets. Today, they seemed okay. The last time she'd seen them, Kelvin had a black eye and a healing scrape on his cheek, while DeAndre looked angry and resigned at the same time.

There was just enough in DeAndre's hand for a large cup of coffee. She knew the boys often stayed awake to avoid falling asleep someplace unsafe. Mella looked over her shoulder and placed the usual order. "Two coffees and two bagels with cream cheese."

Kelvin grimaced and finally spoke. "Ms. Davis, we don't have enough for that." It was his usual demur, this show of pride.

"You can pay me next time you come in."

They only came into the café once or twice a week, always together, always respectful. By habit, Mella gave them more than they paid for. She wanted to make sure they were at least fed while they waited out their time at the youth shelter nearby.

DeAndre, the more charming of the two, gave her a smile and his thanks. What she did for them wasn't nearly enough. Which was why Mella was glad she'd connected with Nala to make Sanctuary a reality. It would be a place where kids like DeAndre and Kelvin could call home without worrying about safety or losing their few belongings. They were sweet kids, and no matter what they had done, short of murder, they didn't deserve to be on the streets and vulnerable to predators lurking in the shadows.

Once the boys got their bagels and coffee, they wandered out of the store toward the path leading down to the beach. Mella put the register back in Colin's hands and returned to Victor and Kingsley's table.

"Sorry about that," she said, reclaiming her tea mug.

"There's no need to apologize for being kind." Victor's voice was low and rough. And there was something new in his eyes that promised to keep her warm inside for the rest of the day.

Mella toyed with the handle of her mug, tongue-tied for what felt like the first time in her life.

Kingsley chuckled over his cup of coffee. "I would tell you guys to get a room, but I think Victor just might take me up on that."

Mella felt her face warm, but played it off with a cheeky smile. "Now, is that anything to say to a lady?"

"To this particular lady, yes," Kingsley said. "I know you won't take advantage of my friend here. He's delicate, you know."

Victor directed a dry smile at his friend, but otherwise didn't dispute anything Kingsley said.

The idea of a delicate Victor made something inside her purr. How delicious it would be to unwrap his prickly exterior to find that alleged fragile thing that few were privy to. Never mind that this wasn't something she had ever looked for in a man before.

Mella took a sip of her tea, fanning her lashes low to hide her eyes. Beside her, Kingsley gave her a knowing look but said nothing else.

Chapter 6

Victor didn't know how he ended up in his kitchen on a Saturday afternoon, cooking for two while anticipatory tension simmered in him. Well, he knew exactly how it had happened, actually. Kingsley had opened his big mouth and invited Mella over. Would his friend ever stop meddling in his life? *Maybe that's the only way you'd actually have a life*, a traitorous part of his brain responded.

Before he'd left Mella's café, they'd agreed for her to come over a few days later at four in the afternoon. Late enough in the day for him to get work done before she arrived.

After going to Sanctuary, then the gym, he spent the rest of the afternoon cooking. Unlike anything else in his life, cooking calmed him. The rhythm of his knife against the cutting board was like meditation. The scent of fresh ginger as he broke open the root and exposed it to air and light was better than the sweetest perfume.

His father had taught him to cook, and Victor supplemented what he taught him with a subscription to half a dozen cooking magazines. He preferred experimentation instead of tried-and-true recipes—the only area of his life where he was prone to fly by the seat of his pants.

Speaking of pants… He glanced at his watch and realized he only had another hour before Mella would arrive. It was just enough time to take a shower and change out of his jeans and T-shirt while the chicken gumbo simmered on low heat. The kitchen smelled spicy and sweet from the combined scents of the gumbo, the olive-and-cheese focaccia staying warm in the oven and the cherry pie.

He needed to make his hour count. After a quick stir to the simmering pot of gumbo, he took off his apron and folded it over one of the four bar stools bracketing the kitchen island. He was leaving the kitchen to head for the shower when the doorbell rang. Victor looked at his watch.

No. It couldn't be her this early.

But when he opened the door, Mella stood on his front step with her hair thick and wild around her face, her smile a bit tamer around the edges.

What are you doing here so early? was what he didn't say. He was too stunned by her to say anything at all. All he could do was stare and pull the door open wider, a wordless invitation to come in.

She was dressed in yellow, a bright canary dress that brought out the light in her dark skin. The dress was spring itself, fitted to her slender torso and flared at the hips. Her high heels were an explosion of color. Green, red and blue flowers. The look of her, brown skin hugged tight in yellow silk, made him think of sex in a sun-drenched bedroom. His bedroom.

It took a moment to realize she was staring at him, too. Right. She'd never seen him wearing anything except the black slacks and shirt combination he found easiest to maintain when not at home. He was still wearing old jeans and the pale gray Mensa T-shirt Violet had given him the year she died.

Victor tried not to shift beneath Mella's intent gaze. He hoped he was at least a little successful. Those eyes of hers could eat a man alive.

"Hi," she said. "I was dressed and ready like, three hours ago. So I thought I might put myself out of my misery and just come over."

The admission of nervousness was endearing and broke the spell he was under.

"You look beautiful," he finally said after staring at her like an idiot for far too long.

"Thank you." Mella ducked her head in a show of shyness he never expected from her.

He closed the front door once she was in the foyer and guided her through the house to the kitchen.

"Would you like something to drink? Water? Wine? Something else?"

She leaned into the marble countertop of the kitchen island with a slow smile, her hip perched on a stool. Her lipstick was purple. "Some water, please."

It was slightly unnerving how easily she fit into his house. She was a burst of color in his kitchen, sunlight pouring through the floor-to-ceiling windows to worship her skin and starburst hair. Mella had never been more beautiful to him.

Damn Kingsley to hell.

Victor poured her a glass of water, then went to the stove to unnecessarily look under the lid of the gumbo pot. With his back to her, he shrugged to shake the nervousness from his shoulders.

"I was about to take a shower."

She looked him over, then slid from the bar stool, a faint smile on her lips. Victor stood at the stove, watching with tense anticipation as she came closer to him. Mella's smile slowly faded from her face with each step until, only inches away from him, her smile disappeared altogether. She tilted her head up, sniffed his throat and bent her head to nose indelicately into his armpit.

"You smell fine. Better than fine, in fact." She stepped back, once again wearing that smile of hers. "I wish all the chefs or cooks or whoever made my meals smelled as good as you do."

"What? Like raw ass, or five hours in the kitchen?"

Her brows jerked up and she grinned. "If that's what raw ass smells like, I may have to change my diet."

The shock of her words ran through him. He swallowed hard, wanting suddenly and desperately to make that vision of her, naked and heaving in his bed under the rain of sunlight, a reality.

"I've changed my mind," she said with her back to him and her skirt swaying with each step. "I *will* have some of your 'something else.'"

"Okay." He could handle that.

At the kitchen island, he measured and mixed the drink he'd carefully researched before buying the ingredients—red vodka, amaretto almond liqueur, peach schnapps and juice from a blood orange. He mixed them in a shaker with ice and poured the drink in a chilled wineglass.

"That looks and smells yummy," Mella said, tapping the long-stemmed glass with a curious finger. "What is it?"

"Love Potion Number 99."

Her eyebrows danced up and she smiled, full of mischief. "Should I be scared to drink it?"

"Only if the idea of falling in love with me frightens you."

A look flashed across Mella's face. He was too polite to call it "frozen terror," but it was damn close. Victor almost smiled. "Don't worry. It's no bite and all bark. You said you like to try new things. I thought this would intrigue you." He slid the glass closer to her. "Go ahead. Taste."

She looked skeptical. "Am I going to wake up naked in a strange bed with no memory of how I got there?"

"Not with me you won't. When I make love to you, I'll make sure you're aware of every single moment." He actually hadn't meant to say that. Out loud.

Mella's eyes flashed wide, and then she looked down, hiding her expression with a sweep of her lashes. Subtle color brushed her cheeks, and Victor wanted to touch her skin to feel the sudden warmth rising there. Then she looked up, and the shyness was gone. She reached for the glass and put it to her purple painted lips, drank with a sensuous movement of her throat.

"It's strong." She blew out a peach-scented breath. "Strong but good."

"Like any decent love potion should be." Victor nodded in satisfaction, then quickly disposed of the empty shaker and the juiced half of the blood orange.

Mella watched him as he returned to lean on the granite counter across from her, wiping his hands with a small towel. "You're not having any?"

"No," he said. "I don't drink."

"Ah."

He paused, waiting for her to ask why, to pick at the painful scab of his sister's death. Although he never told Patrice the real reason, that question had been one of the first things she asked him when they started seeing each other, inquiring with a scandalized widening of her eyes why he drank ginger ale and sparkling water all the time.

But Mella only shrugged, fingers toying with the ends of her twist-out curls. "Okay. I'll enjoy this love potion for both of us." She slid the stem of the delicate crystal between her index and middle fingers, swirling the deep red liquid in the glass before taking a sip. "Yummy."

Victor released the breath he hadn't realized he was

holding. But when Mella hummed in pleasure as she savored the taste of the cocktail on her tongue, another kind of tension held him stiff. Victor's pants suddenly felt uncomfortable. He thanked whatever impulse had led him to stand on the other side of the kitchen island. He surreptitiously adjusted himself in his jeans.

"So, tell me—" Mella murmured with a smile that said she was still thinking about the cocktail's flavor in her mouth "—what are you cooking?"

Cooking? Oh yeah... He felt off balance and desperately aroused. All from a wet-lipped smile and lips clutched at the rim of a wineglass.

Taking two years off from sex now seemed like the worst idea he'd ever had. He cleared his throat, twisting his hands in the kitchen towel to stop himself from reaching for her.

"I have chicken gumbo with brown rice, bread and pie," he managed to say without disgracing himself.

Mella leaned closer with a pleased smile. "Hmm." Her lashes fluttered low over her eyes. "I love multicourse meals."

Was she even talking about food now? Victor put the kitchen towel down and forced himself to relax. This wasn't the first time he'd wanted a woman he had no intention of taking. But damn, Mella was making it hard for him. In his sunlit kitchen, she was warm and sensuous, her body a graceful and tilting thing toward him, an alluring invitation. Each time the wineglass moved away from her lips, it revealed a smile. That smile was sunshine and seduction all at once. Mella had to know what she was doing to him.

Enough of this. Victor pushed himself away from the kitchen island, the marble cool beneath his palms. "Come." He touched her arm.

She left her wineglass and followed him to one of the stoves where the gumbo simmered in a big cast-iron pot. He waited until she was close, her breath a warm exhalation on his arm, before he swept off the cover. She drew in a startled breath, her posture of the irresistible siren abruptly gone.

"This smells incredible!"

"And I hope it tastes even better." He pulled back to allow her to peer in and see the delicate bubbles swelling in the dense bed of shredded chicken, turkey sausage and garlic.

She touched him, a hot palm against the back of his arm. His muscles twitched. "Can I taste it?"

Victor imagined briefly, the weakness overtaking him, that she was talking about something else. He took a single step back from her and somehow found a spoon without burning himself. Steadying the wooden spoon, he dipped it into the gumbo and lifted it toward her mouth. After a startled glance at him, she parted her lips.

"Oh my God." Her groan of appreciation almost undid him. "This is ridiculous."

"Good?"

"No. Not good. Damn amazing." She licked the empty spoon. "How have you not ravished this entire pot by yourself? This is ambrosia."

"Luckily I've had a taste before." He put another

spoonful to her mouth. "This is for you to enjoy any way that you wish."

Victor couldn't stop the low rumble of his voice. Yes, all this was a metaphor. What Vivian had said to him a few days before at the restaurant made him re-evaluate his intentions toward Mella. Yes, she was a largely unknown entity, though obviously a wild arbor to his trimmed hedges. But he still wanted her so badly that it hurt.

"Thank you for this." Mella licked the spoon again, her pink tongue leaving a wet trail on the long brown wood.

A choked sound left his throat, and he eased his hips back away from hers, achingly aware of his own arousal. It seemed then that she finally realized how close they were standing, and how obscenely she was licking the empty spoon. She blushed and pulled away from the spoon as if it was on fire. It clattered into the sink.

"My pleasure." He cleared his throat. "It's almost ready." He grabbed the cooking spoon and stirred the pot again for want of something to do with his hands that didn't involve peeling the clothes off her body.

"Is it?" She went back to get her drink. With her glass in hand, she leaned against the kitchen island. "I get the feeling if Kingsley hadn't pushed, you wouldn't have invited me over here." There was teasing in her voice, but a thread of seriousness, too.

"I would have," he said. "Eventually."

Her arched brow was all doubt. He took a breath and poured himself some ginger ale, sat on the stool across from her and curved his hand around the cold glass that clinked with ice.

"For a while, I'd been thinking about a do-over." He paused to consider his words carefully, but a flutter of her fingers in the air urged him to keep going. "You came to my office with an invitation to lunch, to thank me. But it's me who should be thanking you."

"Meaning?"

"Sanctuary is an incredible project. Without you, I would've never been involved in it, so thank you. Helping these kids is good work. It's messed up that they got kicked out of their homes for whatever reason. Parenting has no expiration date. There are no conditions under which your child no longer becomes worthy of your love. It's criminal some people don't realize that."

Mella nodded. "I agree. When Nala and I started talking about Sanctuary, it seemed like the perfect fit. During the school year, I'm a volunteer math and science teacher at the Y. Homeless kids sometimes come to me for help with their schoolwork. They were still trying to do right by themselves despite not having a place to live. It breaks my heart that they're out there and have few places or people to turn to." Her mouth hovered over her wineglass, and her eyes darted away from him. "When I was eight, my parents died and my aunt rescued me. She took me into her home and gave me a good life. That's something I want to do for young people, to provide a home when the one they'd known all their lives is suddenly gone."

Mella frowned into her glass, mouth curved down in a way that made him want to gather her into his arms.

For the first time since they'd met, she looked vulnerable. That touched something in him.

"Sometimes we all need to be rescued," he said. "It's a good thing there are people out there in the world in their invisible suits of armor doing the work that needs to be done."

She bit her lip and smiled at him, a self-conscious dimple in her cheek. Victor wanted to slide a hand across the table and comfort her, make her know that if she ever needed it, he would come to her rescue again and again. She would never need to call; he would simply be there.

The impulse made him frown and pull back. He'd never felt that before. Suddenly, he felt like he was drowning.

What was Mella doing to him?

Chapter 7

Across from Mella, Victor cleared his throat. He pulled slightly back from her, then as if reconsidering, settled back onto the speckled burgundy granite, forearms braced, fingers linked. "Being able to pay a rescue forward is something few are able to do. You're very lucky." Victor's mouth was still the shape of seduction and self-control. There was nothing of pity in him. Which was what made Mella want to keep talking.

She swirled the drink in her glass, not looking at him, only seeing the scarlet truth serum stirring in the delicate crystal.

"My parents died when I was eight," she said. "They were walking together when they were run over by a car." The truth of her past spilled out like blood, staining what had been an easy afternoon in Victor's brightly lit kitchen. "My aunt took me in when I felt the most alone."

"She must be a remarkable and patient woman." His unexpected remark teased a smile out of her.

"Yes, she is." Mella took another sip of her drink, savoring its heady flavor. Was it a love potion or sweetened truth serum? Either way, she'd never felt more attracted to Victor, or more soothed by his presence, than in that moment.

Away from everyone else, it was easy to talk to him. She'd forgotten. His house was cozy and warm, a surprising mix of handmade wooden furniture and warm fabrics. Rugs on the floor, a burgundy-and-gold tapestry hanging along the entire back wall of the living room they'd walked through. She'd expected glass and harsh modern lines, geometry and display cases masquerading as furniture, but what she got was so much better.

It was humbling how much she had misjudged him. This serious man also cooked joyous meals. This logical architect listened while she wailed about her savior complex. It was easier to think about those things rather than dwell on the attraction between them that made her consider more than a no-strings affair.

"Your aunt also raised a remarkable woman of her own."

Mella pulled herself back from her thoughts, ran the conversation over in her mind to find the thread she'd abandoned. "What? I'm not patient, too?"

"Let's not get carried away here."

"You wouldn't say that if you knew how long I've

been waiting to get into your pants." She clapped her hand over her mouth when she realized what she said. "Damn! I mean, I'm looking forward to tasting what you have tonight." She dropped her face into her hands and groaned in embarrassment. *What are you doing, Michaela?* She peeked up at him, hoping he didn't think she was too much of an idiot.

The smile lurking around Victor's mouth became an outright laugh. The corners of his sloe eyes crinkled with mirth, and the sound of his joy took up every bit of space in the kitchen.

"It's okay," he said when his laughter tapered off to occasional chuckles. "Do you want another?" He gestured to her nearly empty glass.

She shook her head, cheeks still hot with mortification. "At the rate I'm going, I need to cut myself off now."

"No need to be embarrassed. The feeling is mutual. Which I'm sure you know."

Yes, she was *very* aware that her attraction wasn't one-sided. Between the kiss they'd shared at his office and the way he flirted with her at the café, Mella knew very much he wanted her, too. But desire wasn't enough, was it? Not when they ultimately wanted different things from their possible physical connection.

Mella reached out for her glass, ignoring the tremor in her hand. It would be a shame not to enjoy the last drop of such a delicious concoction. She tipped the last of it in her mouth, savoring its sweet bite on her tongue.

Before she could put the empty glass on the counter, Victor took it from her with the barest brush of their fingers. Electricity jolted between them, a flash-ing heat that singed down into her lap. Mella bit her lip and watched him take the glass to the sink, fasci-nated by his effortlessly powerful body and the way he wielded it for the most mundane of tasks. She could easily imagine how he was in bed. By turns tender and fierce, muscles sliding with sweat under her grasp-ing hands.

Jesus... She needed to get her imagination under control.

"Do you work out?" The words slipped from her mouth, pushed out of her by the stretch of his muscles under the thin T-shirt.

Victor lifted the cover of the cast-iron pot to stir the gumbo. He didn't hide his smile. "A little. Not as much as I used to. More to soothe any mental restlessness that being in the kitchen can't take care of."

She wondered how often he was restless and why. "I spar at the Y downtown. Kickboxing. That soothes me sometimes."

Something flickered behind the mask she suspected he always wore. "Really? I do a little myself." His eye skated over her body. It was a disconcertingly intimate look that made her shiver, despite knowing it was only spurred by his surprise at her not looking like the typi-cal kickboxer.

"Don't look so shocked," she said. "I can take you down any day of the week."

His eyebrow rose again, and now there was defi-nitely amusement directed her way. Mella thought he would say something about her size or her femininity.

But he surprised her yet again. "Any day? How about next Wednesday?"

"You're on, Mr. Raphael." She grinned. "Prepare to lose."

"I'll try to prepare myself for anything." His mouth twitched again with amusement. "Time for dinner." The cast iron clattered when he closed the pot.

He served the meal at the kitchen island instead of the dining room table. Although the granite surface was already clean, he wiped it down again and put out the place settings, all the while insisting that she just sit and do nothing.

"You're a guest. Guests aren't supposed to be put to work," he said. "Just be warned, the next time you come over, you won't be a guest anymore."

"I'll bring my own apron, then."

Once the places were set, he brought out a platter of brown rice, two bowls of gumbo and a loaf of focaccia bread already sliced and releasing its delectable steam into the air.

"Oh my God, what's that?" She leaned over the bread and inhaled. "Did you bake that today?"

"Of course." He looked pleased. "Olive and Asiago focaccia for my first guest in many, many months." He put the bread, diagonally sliced to show melted white cheese and thin slices of green and black olives, to rest on a narrow piece of wood.

Mella clasped her hands in anticipation. "This is going to be *so* good."

"Don't say that when you haven't even tasted anything yet."

"It smells like my birthday in here. Of course everything is going to be good."

Good turned out to be an understatement.

With an entire bowl of her own, the gumbo slid over her tongue like a dream of ambrosia. Having simmered nearly an hour since her taste test, it was even better. Salty and meaty, the scent seduced her nose before she put her mouth around the spoon and allowed her tongue to taste. Mella was moaning before she even swallowed the first bite. Victor watched her, a smile, small as it was, curving his hard mouth.

"Good?"

"The best I've ever had."

She couldn't say anything coherent for the rest of the meal. When Victor pulled apart the already sliced and hot pieces of fresh-baked bread, she swore her knees grew weak. If she hadn't been sitting on the stool, she would have fallen where she was. The bread's crust was firm and flaky, giving way to the soft and doughy center. The slices of olives were perfect circles of salt-laced flavor, the melted Asiago cheese loosening yet another moan from her throat.

"How are you not married?" she demanded with her last bite of bread perched between two fingers.

"Because my cooking only makes up for so many of my deficiencies."

"Any man who can cook like this doesn't have any deficiencies in my book." Mella held her piece of bread in one hand, the spoon dipping into the bowl of gumbo with the other. "This is honestly the best meal I've had in a long time, if ever." She couldn't stop talking about the food, or eating it. "If I'd known you could throw down like this in the kitchen, I'd have asked you to make the kids a meal their first night in Sanctuary, not redesign the damn grounds."

"Who says I can't do both?" The sincerity in his face made her want to jump across the counter and hug him.

"You don't have to do that," she said.

"What if I want to?"

"Then I won't stop you."

"Good."

Although she didn't think it was possible, the warmth of his look made the food in Mella's mouth taste even better. "Thank you, Victor. You're really amazing."

"And you haven't even had dessert yet."

"Dessert?" Her hand hovered over the last piece of bread on the serving board. "Oh, I'd forgotten there was more."

"With me, there's always more."

She loved that he was in a teasing mood. "Amen and hallelujah to that." Mella smiled around another spoonful of gumbo and pulled the bowl even closer.

So good...

She didn't pay the strictest attention to everything Victor said while she ate. All Mella knew for sure was that the food was good, and he was still in the same room with her, and his micro smiles kept coming. The happiness built so quickly in her, it was almost scary. But she released that fear and allowed herself to just enjoy the food and the company.

Before too long, she swallowed the last bite of

gumbo and purposely pushed away from the counter. Her stomach felt pleasantly full but not tight from over-satisfaction.

"I think you've ruined me for other people's food."

"I don't mind that at all." He leaned over to refill her water glass.

The sun was getting lower in the sky, a brilliant blast of color that poured in through the open windows. Although she hadn't really appreciated it before, the view from the kitchen was truly spectacular. Victor might not claim to be rich, but he had some of the most beautiful real estate in Miami that a "regular guy" could have. The rippling blue water of Biscayne Bay was calm and blue just beyond the windows. A large boat sailed placidly by while the outlines of the city rose into the clouds, Miami in blue.

"This is the tastiest meal I've had in a long time," she said. "Thank you."

"I should be the one thanking you for coming over. I wasn't sure you'd make it." He winced then, like the honesty of the words pained him.

"Why? You invited me and I accepted."

"I assumed you would rather be partying with your friends." *Like the day I met you*, was the unspoken comment. "Maybe clubbing or lazing at a beachside brunch spot."

Mella shrugged, not apologizing for the things she enjoyed. "I'm meeting up with my girls later on this evening. No sense in letting a Saturday night go to waste." She took a sip of her water and swallowed it with a pleased sigh. Even his damn *water* tasted divine.

"But I like other things aside from clubs and drinking and meeting up with gorgeous men in bars." She raised teasing eyebrows at him. Victor tipped his head in acknowledgment, his mouth curving up. "If we get to know each other better, you'll see that I enjoy relaxing with a glass of wine and good conversation just as much as I do a good party."

Victor was thoughtful. He nodded slowly. "I look forward to that."

Meaningful silence hovered between them, moments when Mella bit the inside of her lip and thought about what they had both just hinted at. A long-term thing. More afternoons like this. Them getting to know each other more than just on the surface. But this wasn't what she wanted, was it? She jumped up from the stool to pick up the plates and take them toward the sink. Victor intercepted her, a large hand on her wrist before she could grab her own plate.

"You're a guest, remember?"

At that moment, she couldn't remember much of anything. He was so close. The breath she drew smelled completely of him—the spices from the gumbo embedded in his clothes, the faint salt of sweat on his skin. The remnants of some sort of deodorant. Mella shivered from her awareness of him.

Her hands released the hold on the plate, and the heavy white porcelain dropped back to the place mat with a thud.

"Damn!" She jerked back from the granite counter, fully expecting the bowl to break.

"It's all right," he said, his breath hot against her lips. "Nothing is broken."

But that wasn't quite true. Any half-made resolve to not let her hormones control the afternoon shattered with the touch of his mouth on hers. His lips were dry and warm, a light pressure, something she could refuse or accept. He pulled back and she drew in an unsteady breath, licked her lips while vague thoughts of staying on her side of the kitchen island went largely ignored. Mella chased his retreating mouth with her own.

She wanted more.

He made a sound of triumph and licked her mouth. She hissed at the sensuous wetness of him, the firm shape of his lips against hers, his tongue teasing her mouth open.

Mella sighed and let him in, although they were both chasing the pleasure of mouth-to-mouth contact. He gave and she took. She chased, and he acquiesced. It was nothing like their first kiss in his office. This one was more intimate, made even more so by the fact that they were in his house, in his kitchen, with his food in her belly.

"Damn, you're a good kisser."

She panted the words to nullify the overwhelming feeling of *more* and *closer* and *please* that filled her up. This was what she had chased. This was the feeling she wanted. It was not Victor's fault that it was at once too much, but also not enough. Men were disposable. Someone who kissed like this, who made her feel such overwhelming want and surrender, was not.

But Victor kissed away her objections, curved his

hand around the back of her neck and drew her closer. She whimpered at the drowning heat that filled her, flooding from the contact point between their bodies to pool between her legs.

This is just a kiss, she thought frantically. *Just a kiss*.

Except that it wasn't. Mella gripped his shoulders, could only hold on as their tongues licked and stroked, drenching her from the inside out. The edge of the granite island pressed into her back the same moment his hands moved to cup her face.

She felt warm, then hot, her entire body building toward a familiar tension that promised to lead to something she wanted very much. The aching sweetness of it made her gasp and wriggle against him. But even as he held her close, he also held her firmly away, only their chests and mouths touching. Mella thought she knew why. She mewled in her throat.

No, he wasn't allowed to withhold that from her. She wanted that, too. She hooked her fingers into his belt loops and pulled him closer.

Yes. God, yes.

She sighed with satisfaction at the feel of him full and hard against her stomach. He trembled against her, pulled back, his mouth wet and parted, eyes nearly black with lust.

"I want you."

He wasn't asking permission. He wasn't saying he would take her. But it was a combination of both those things, and that made Mella's knees weak. She sagged back into the cool granite, licking her lips. "How badly do you want me?"

Victor growled. He honest-to-God growled in the back of his throat and swooped down to kiss her again. She thought his kisses were intense before, but now…now he devoured. The sweetness, the politeness blinked out of existence. He snaked his tongue against her own, thumbed her nipple to encourage her to catch up.

But Mella was already there. She writhed against him, searching for more stimulation, wallowing in the touch of his hands that were everywhere as he crowded even more into her space, his sex hard and insistent against her belly. She shivered with the urgent sweep of his tongue, chasing the pleasure he obviously took in pleasing her. She circled her hips against his. And he shuddered again, a gasping breath exploding from him as if he'd just been punched in the stomach. He groaned a curse against her mouth, slid a hand down to her thigh.

Yes…

Her body screamed its permission as his hand slipped under the wide skirt. Her thighs fell open, and she hissed at the first touch of his fingers between her legs. Mella jerked against him, her hands flying back to balance against the edge of the counter. It made her quiver and squirm, that slow stroke up the inside of her thigh where she'd expected him to simply dive into the place where she was wet and aching.

"Stop teasing," she gasped.

His hot laugh was a surprise, hand curling around her bare hip under the dress, pulling her hard against him.

"You smell delicious," he rumbled.

"Then eat me." It came out as a demand.

But he shook his head, pulled back to nibble on her lower lip, kiss the corners of her mouth. She was damn near about to wriggle out of her skin. She was swollen and wet, had been since the first press of his mouth to hers. And now, in the midst of the fifth or fiftieth kiss, it felt as if she would float away on the river of lust flooding between her thighs. But the gentleness of his kisses now seemed intent on calming her down. Even though his kisses were light and soft and nibbling, conveying a deep hunger without the rush to sate it, the hand between her legs was anything but leisurely. He gripped her hip harder and pulled her rhythmically against him.

"Oh God!" Her head dropped back, too heavy to hold up. Mella bared her neck to him, breathing harshly through her parted lips.

Victor's rough afternoon beard rubbed her throat and the line of her shoulder as he nibbled her ear, licked the curving shell. And it was even more inciting because of the hand she couldn't see under her skirt. She could only feel it, the drag of his blunt nails up her inner thigh, and then a finger, one single finger, stroking her through her panties: a steady up-and-down caress that pushed every rational thought from her head. She opened her legs wider for him, feeling absolutely whorish under his steady attentions.

He kissed and licked her collarbone above the neckline of her dress, making her feel both treasured and desired, safe in a way she'd never experienced before with any man. The difference between what he was doing to her above her waist versus below was driving her insane. His finger slid beneath the fabric of her panties and she cried in relief.

At last yes, at last!

His finger slid along the wet crevice of her, stroking and teasing. Then it was two fingers, then easing inside. His thumb flicked the hard button of her pleasure.

Oh God…

She wanted to beg him. She wanted to surge down and swallow those fingers with her woman's flesh, force him to go faster and leap toward the destination of bliss he so skillfully promised. But he held her against the counter in a firm and unyielding grip that only allowed her to circle her hips. She whimpered his name. A plea. But it only made him go slower, feeding her the inches of his fingers until she was sobbing his name and wanting more. His thumb tapped wetly against her clitoris and she whimpered.

"Vict—"

The heat of arousal crawled through Mella's thighs, the seat of her sex, overwhelming and so, so good. She wanted to share with him how wonderful it felt, how amazing to see her world on the edge of implosion. She reached out for him, sacrificing her hold on the edge of the counter to tug at his jeans. The thick weight of him pressed into her palm through the denim. She moaned as he twitched against her fingers. Victor firmly pushed her hand away.

"Let me…" He breathed the words into the skin of her bared shoulder, sucked a bruise into her neck while his hand made love to her, no *took* her under her skirt.

It was slow and methodical, his fingers sliding into
her, twisting and curving, brushing against that spot
inside her that made her sob out loud, gasp and come
so close to screaming his name.

Victor bit her throat and whispered hot filth into
her ear.

"I want to be inside you." He bit her throat. "But it's
been so long, I'd explode if you…ah!…even touch me."
Victor panted against her neck. "But you'd like that,
wouldn't you?" He groaned into her skin, his breath
scorching. "You'd love it." His fingers were merciless
under her skirt.

Mella didn't know she could feel so much at once.
The heat of lust, the sweetness of his mouth on her skin
that almost felt like love. Their breaths panted loud in
the kitchen. Desire and want and desperation all hung
on the tips of his fingers curling up inside her to—

"Oh my God!"

Her world burst open with light. It was a long while
before she could even remember her own name. She
shivered in the shelter of Victor's arms as she came
down from her high, her entire world still crackling
with fireworks behind her tightly closed eyelids. Mella
opened her eyes to find her forehead pressed into his
chest. Her throat was hoarse. Her legs shook from their
precarious balance on the floor.

Slowly, Victor pulled back, steadying her with hands
around her waist. Mella licked her lips. This was fine.
She could do this. With hands that shook, she reached
for his zipper again, but he clasped her hands in his
and pulled her fully to her feet.

"Are you ready for dessert?"

If she hadn't been paying such close attention to him over the past few weeks, she wouldn't have noticed the change in his voice, the deeper register of it, the faint tremor. He wanted her. As badly as she did, he wanted her to get on her knees for him. But why wouldn't he let her? She licked her lips.

"I think I've already had my dessert," she said. "And it was spectacular."

"I aim to please."

Apparently.

Victor cleared his throat. "I'll be right back."

He excused himself, and Mella watched him go with both relief and regret, collapsing into the counter at her back. Her thighs still trembled, and she felt sticky and wet. This was just attraction, she told herself with a mental shake. *Stop acting like you've never had a man give you a damn orgasm before.* Because she'd had her share, but not a single one of them had denied themselves the reciprocal attention she was more than happy to supply. If he was in the bathroom jerking—

"You can use the bathroom if you like." He came back into the kitchen drying his hands on a towel, the bulge in his jeans less obvious but still there. "There are plenty of towels and soaps there."

Mella blushed and yanked her gaze back to his face. "Thanks, I think I will."

She quickly closed and locked the bathroom door behind her, leaning into the cool wood as she allowed herself to tremble and blink quickly at nothing without the danger of being seen.

Oh my God...

After he'd made her come, she practically had to scoop her brains off the floor and pour them back into her head. Even now she was completely useless. A noise outside the door made her jump. Okay. She needed to get it together. No use having him think she'd fallen in or something equally embarrassing.

Quickly, Mella cleaned herself, then washed her hands in the sink. But even after she was done, her face still looked sweaty and overheated. As if she'd just had one of the best orgasms of her life on top of Victor's kitchen island.

After washing her face and reapplying lotion and her light makeup, she looked a lot better. But she still felt like a pile of wilted noodles. When she was ready, she left the bathroom. She paused in the entryway of the kitchen to watch Victor carefully take a pie from the oven.

The pie smelled like baked cherries, hot doughy crust and something vaguely nutty. Mouthwatering. The scent of the dessert was delicious, but it was Victor she couldn't stop staring at. He was so perfect, his body a photographer's dream under the nearly transparent gray shirt and faded black jeans. He was still barefoot and his feet were long and wide, braced against the honey-colored kitchen tiles as he skillfully handled the glass baking dish. He slid the pie onto a cooling rack. Mella could watch him forever.

Her breath caught. What? Her hands clenched into her skirt, and she swayed in the doorway. No. Thoughts of forever were not in this equation. This was supposed to be fun. Nothing "forever" about it. The last time she had assumed forever, her parents had been killed and gutted from her life, a cruel surgery she had never recovered from. She couldn't do that to herself. She just couldn't.

"I—"

Victor turned at the sound of her voice, a look of expectation on his face, a hint of a smile. "Can't wait?" He pulled off the oven mitts and dropped them on the counter.

Mella shook her head. "No, it's not that. I—"

She knew the words that needed to come out of her mouth, knew that the quicker she said them, the easier it would be in the long run. She took two steps back, a hand braced against the wall.

"I...forgot there's something else I need to do." Mella took the coward's way out and forced the lie past her lips. "I have to go."

His expression blanked. "Okay."

No. Mella wanted to scream. She wanted the playful Victor again. The one who made sexual innuendos while feeding her gumbo and promising her the most delicious dessert she'd ever had in her life. But this cold man was the Victor she deserved. Mella bit the inside of her lip.

"I'll just—I'll just see myself out." And before Victor could leave the kitchen, she turned and walked quickly toward the front door. Her heels clattered against the marble floors as she hurried through the house. She grabbed the door handle and wrenched at it. But it didn't open. Mella gave a cry of frustration and yanked it again. Tears of panic burned behind her eyes. "Goddammit!"

A big hand curled over hers the same moment she felt a furnace of warmth at her back. Victor's finger pressed a button on the handle, and she heard the low sound of a lock disengaging. She couldn't look at him. But she couldn't be rude.

"Thank you."

"You're welcome." His voice was low and flat.

Mella scurried away like a coward to her car. She felt Victor's gaze on her the whole way, a prickle of awareness between her shoulder blades, but she didn't turn to look at the ruin she had caused. She couldn't.

Chapter 8

The day of the Sanctuary unveiling came much too quickly for Mella. During the time between the dinner at Victor's place and the party, she and Victor had communicated mostly by email and one memorably bland phone call that was all business. The times she and Nala had gone to the mansion to check on the work, it was Victor's coworker, Brianne, who showed them around. Brianne had been polite and professional, but Mella could tell she had no idea what she was doing there instead of her boss.

Oblivious to the awkward undertones of the inspection, Nala sang praises to Victor's skill and timeliness. Only a few details needed to be changed, and a conversation with Brianne handled that easily enough. The weeks passed by, and then Sanctuary was ready.

Mella wished she was less of a coward about facing Victor, but she just couldn't do it. He was everything she wanted, and that was dangerous.

The night of the grand-opening party, she stared at her reflection, wearing the dress Nala insisted on buying for her in thanks for helping to make Sanctuary a reality. The dress was nothing Mella would have bought for herself, purely because the price tag was laughable.

But a few weeks before, when they'd walked Lincoln Road Mall after a lunch meeting, Nala must have seen the way she practically had eye sex with the designer dress. Less than a week later, it was being delivered to her office at Café Michaela with a note saying the dress had been altered to fit Mella's measurements and couldn't be returned.

Mella turned in front of the floor-length mirror, the Roberto Cavalli cocktail dress clinging to her shape and emphasizing the tuck of her waist and her long legs. The dress was perfect, an elegant green-and-yellow tropical print of birds on a white background. Mella checked out the back view. Very nice. She was well aware that focusing on the dress mostly stopped her from thinking about Victor and the possibility that he would be at the party. Mostly. She jerked away from her reflection when the phone rang.

"I'm in the driveway." Her aunt's voice came through the phone.

"I'll be right down."

Mella grabbed her purse and tucked the phone away.

After another quick glance at her reflection, she went out to meet her aunt.

"You look like you're ready for the runway in that." Her aunt, dressed in a tuxedo and with her hair braided into a silver-and-black Nefertiti crown, opened the door of the Lexus convertible for Mella.

"I'm dressed for a fancy mansion party." Mella willed her tension away and climbed into the passenger seat. "Just trying to look the part."

Her aunt's gaze narrowed. "Is it a gift from that boy you can't get out of your head?"

She winced but tried to hide it, grabbing on to a light and carefree mood with both hands. "No, not from Victor. Nala."

"Ah." If possible, Aunt Jess looked even more suspicious. "Is she trying to…?"

"No, nothing like that." Mella buckled her seat belt as the car pulled out of her driveway. "I'm shocked you'd think just because she's into women that she'd try something with me. *You* don't go after every pretty girl you see."

"I'm different." Aunt Jess turned onto the busy main street when the traffic allowed. "I don't have the type of reputation she has."

"What, as a philanthropist?" Mella couldn't believe her aunt was going there.

Aunt Jess gave another noncommittal shrug and continued driving. "They say she's into all kinds of things."

"Aunt Jess, don't be a gossip. Nala's best friend is a straight woman who she loves like a sister. She's a generous woman giving away her family mansion so homeless kids can have a place to live, for God's sake."

"You only know how things seem, Michaela, not how they are."

"I could tell you the same thing." She was a little shocked at her aunt's suspicions. Of anyone, she assumed her aunt would be the most supportive of what the young billionaire was doing with her money. But Mella also knew what they said about assumptions. They'd make an ass out of you every time.

"What's going on here, Aunt Jess? Do you know something I don't?"

"No. I just don't trust her."

There had to be something else going on, Mella thought with a frown.

"Don't worry about me, honey. Just get your mind right for this party. You've been an emotional mess the last few weeks."

Aunt Jess knew just how to distract her. This time it was with the truth. She made a mental note to ask about this odd mistrust later on. Tonight, she needed to keep it together. This was about Sanctuary and the great work they had all done to make it a reality.

The evening was split into two parts: a congratulatory party for Nala's best friend, Nichelle, with only close friends and family invited, followed by the larger public event. Nala told her that everyone was happy and relieved that Nichelle had (finally, according to their friends and family) married Wolfe, her longtime business partner, and given birth to a child who was unfairly blessed in the stunning-good-looks department. Although she'd never met Nichelle, she'd seen photographs of her in the papers, both by herself and with her gorgeous new husband. They both looked like they stepped out of a European fashion magazine, all good looks, charm and billions of dollars between the two of them.

At ten that night, the party would change and open up to the press, potential donors to Sanctuary's non-profit and to everyone who had a hand in making the mansion into what it was now. This included Victor and the people from his firm.

Mella winced at the thought of him. She ignored her aunt's questioning look, turned on the radio and leaned back to enjoy the rest of the ride.

When they pulled up to the mansion, a suited valet came out to take away their car. She and her aunt got out to the sounds of a Whitney Houston song, "I'm Every Woman," cheerful and loud, pouring from the house.

Sanctuary was well lit. There were lights along the drive and on the front porch that showed off the valets at the small podium. A loose gathering of people were smoking and talking near the burbling water fountain. She heard the vague sounds of conversations in the relative darkness of the grounds. With the music and lights, Sanctuary was a place of pure joy. She took a breath and stepped into the mansion.

It hadn't been furnished the last time she'd let herself in. There had been only the smell of furniture polish on the banisters, the floors gleaming in the gloom of the day and high ceilings that made the mansion seem bigger than it was. Now there was a funky, modern chandelier hanging in the foyer, pop art prints on the walls, a flat-screen TV and shelves full of books. The house felt young and filled with light.

"And she's just giving all this away?" Her aunt looked around, the expression on her face saying she was impressed but trying not to be.

"It's fantastic, isn't it?"

"She's not worried the kids will steal from this place?"

"I doubt that. But she's got other moving parts to this that I'm barely aware of. Security. Taxes. Maintenance. We created a nonprofit just to deal with the house and all the logistics of running it."

Aunt Jess made another impressed noise.

"Are you ready to admit she's awesome yet?"

"It's easy for rich people to give money away, especially when it's a tax write-off."

"Aunt Jess!"

"What? You asked, and I gave my opinion." Her aunt adjusted the flower in her buttonhole and shrugged. "You should go find your friends. I'm going to hunt down the open bar."

Her aunt gave her shoulder a squeeze, then quickly made herself scarce. Mella shook her head, wondering, other than the obvious situation with Shaun, what was going on with her aunt. The sound of footsteps coming up behind her pushed her forward. She followed the sound of a familiar laugh to a drawing room done up in deep burgundy. There was dark wood everywhere, built-in bookcases on three of the walls and another wide bay window looking out onto the grounds. Waiters in dark suits carried trays of drinks and finger food through the crowd.

It had been Nala's laugh she heard. She was chatting with three women, one of whom was Nichelle Wright-Diallo.

"Michaela!" Nala called her over with an enthusiastic wave.

She looked gorgeous in a 1920s-style drop-waist black dress. As she turned, the dress sparkled in the overhead lights, catching in the tiny crystals embedded in the fabric. Knee-high black combat boots completed the outfit.

Nala took Mella's hand. "Michaela, let me introduce you to one of my favorite people in the entire world, and her sisters." The girls who were obviously not Nichelle rolled their eyes and shared an amused laugh. They were apparently used to Nala.

"This is Nichelle." Nala indicated the unforgettable woman by her side. She wore her hair cut low around her model-gorgeous face. Her figure was stunning in a calf-length black dress contoured with gray at the hips to show off her curves.

This woman really just had a baby?

"Good evening, miracle worker." Nichelle grasped Mella's hand in a cool but sincere handshake. "Nala told us all the work you've done to get this place ready."

"Only the exterior," Mella said. "The house was already amazing."

Nichelle grinned over her shoulder at her best friend. "And modest, too."

Nala shook her head. "Too modest, I say." She waved toward a pair of young women, nearly as tall as Nichelle but with none of her bite. "Meet Madalie and Willa, the sisters."

Madalie leaned in to kiss her briefly on the cheek while Willa waved shyly. "We were just getting the party started."

"It looks pretty well started to me." Mella gestured to the large room filled with a few dozen people, some stuck by the chocolate fountain, others gathered around the man who was undoubtedly Nichelle's husband. "Everything looks great."

"I think so, too." An ecstatic smile broke across Nala's face, warming the cashmere brown of her eyes. "I hope the kids love it."

"I'm sure they will." Mella playfully bumped her shoulder. "They'll be here in a couple of hours to tell you so themselves."

For months now, they'd been taking applicants to live in the house, looking for kids who had no place to go, needed help and didn't seem intent on biting off every hand extended their way in support. It had been a complicated process handled by a firm the Sanctuary Foundation hired. The kids would move in the day after the party.

"This is one of the best things I've ever done," Nala said. Her voice was brave and big, but there was suspicious moisture shining in her eyes. "I want to do more stuff like this, help as many kids as I can."

Mella slipped her hand around the other woman's waist. "And you will. This is a good start."

"It is! This place is quite a show."

Mella turned when she heard her aunt speak. Aunt Jess had a glass of whiskey in her hand, looking both handsome and regal in her black suit and silver crown of hair that reflected back the light.

"Not a show, Aunt Jess, it's a—" Her words choked off when she saw the back of Victor's head. She froze. What was he doing here so early?

Her aunt touched her arm. "Everything okay, honey?"

"Um. Yes. I think so."

"That means no." Aunt Jess glanced in the direction of her gaze. She'd never been more grateful that Victor and her aunt had never met.

"It's nothing," she said. "Promise."

But her aunt didn't look appeased. Mella hurriedly introduced her to the other women. It wasn't long before Nichelle's sisters, fascinated by everything about her aunt, led her off to one of the couches to talk about motorcycles and biker babes.

Mella fell back into the rhythm of the conversation with Nichelle and Nala, but her mind wasn't quite in it. She was still hyperaware of Victor in the room. The length of his back under the black dress shirt, the curve of his firm behind under his slacks, those hands that had cooked for her and touched her so intimately. Mella bit the inside of her lip to keep her attention from wandering. But it didn't really help.

"Do you want to go say hello?"

Huh?

Someone, it must have been Nala, touched her hand and brought her attention back to the conversation.

"I'm sorry, what did you say?"

Nala jerked her chin in the general direction of where Victor had been earlier. "I said Victor Raphael is already here. Do you want to go say hello?" Her eyes sparkled with mischief.

Mella shook herself out of her stupor. "I noticed him earlier." She forced a smile. "If anyone, you should be thanking him for how the grounds look. He truly is a miracle worker."

Nala took her arm. "Come on, let's go find him. I've wanted to thank you two at the same time for ages. Now I finally get the chance before everyone else gets here." Mella couldn't tell if the other woman was messing with her, if she knew about whatever it was that was between her and Victor.

"But shouldn't you make the party more about Nichelle than the renovation? There's always time to talk about business." Mella was desperate to avoid Victor. She hoped she sounded more sincere than she felt.

Nichelle, sharp-eyed in her towering bright blue high heels that apparently allowed her to see everything, touched Mella's shoulder. "Yes, that can wait, Nala. For now, let's have some drinks and listen to me go on and on about my delicious husband." The smile she quirked at Mella was faintly self-mocking. But she practically radiated happiness—a satisfied lioness after the hunt. She curved an arm around Mella's shoulder. "What would you like to drink?"

"Just about anything." Mella needed to have a good

amount of liquor in her to face Victor after nearly three weeks of playing cat and mouse, or whatever they were doing.

"Why don't you come with me? I'm sure we can find you something."

Nala gave her a look of surprise. Mella could easily read her expression: *I thought you two didn't know each other.* But Mella shrugged. She just wanted to be on the other side of the room from Victor, so she willingly went off with Nichelle toward God knew where in the house.

The where turned out to be the anteroom that had been set up as a bar. The room chimed with good humor, the clink of glasses and pleasant rumble of conversation. Aside from the front of the house with the valets and smokers, this seemed to be the busiest place at the party.

"Are you sure you want to leave your liquor up to chance?" Nichelle tilted an eyebrow, a trick, it seemed, that everyone could do except Mella. But she made a good point.

Mella thought about the week she'd had, the possibility of seeing Victor sooner than she was ready. "Umm. A Lime Rickey, please."

When she had the cold highball glass in her hand, she took a long sip of the drink. There was much more bourbon than sparkling water in the glass, but she didn't mind. The drink was tart on her tongue, a pleasant bite that made her taste buds spurt moments before the bourbon burned its way down her throat.

Nichelle watched her much too closely for comfort. "Good?"

"Great."

"Does that mean you'll stop avoiding Victor now?"

Mella swallowed against the flare of denial. She shook her head. "Maybe."

Nichelle took a glass of pineapple juice from the bartender and led Mella to a comfortable leather sofa with a view of the front gardens. Even through the glass and shadows of evening, it was obvious how thoroughly and beautifully Victor had transformed the grounds. Sanctuary's grass and gardens would be both gorgeous to look at and fun to play in. Mella hoped the kids loved the results half as much as she did.

In the chair next to Mella's, Nichelle crossed her long legs. "He's a good man, and you seem like a decent enough person."

"I'm trying not to let your compliments go to my head," Mella said drily.

Nichelle grinned with the glass of pineapple juice at her lips. She was so beautiful. Why didn't every man who saw her fall instantly under her spell?

"Wolfe likes your man well enough," Nichelle continued. "And Kingsley, well. He is who he is. With all his faults, he's a pretty good judge of character, and he wouldn't be friends with a man not worth fighting for."

"I'm not much of a fighter."

"And that means you're a coward, then?" Maybe Mella could see why the men didn't just fall at Nichelle's feet. Her tongue was a cruel thing. Mella glanced down at the towering shoes. And her high heels just might be too deadly for any man foolish enough to be at her feet.

Nichelle's red lips curved up. "You like my shoes?"

"They're high as hell. How can you even walk in them without falling on your face?"

"Years of practice." She looked down at the blue velvet stilettos with a fond smile, as if they were attached to a particularly pleasant memory. "You should go talk to Victor."

"Why do you care?" Mella knew she was sulking, but just didn't know what to do about it yet.

Nichelle sat silent for a moment, leaning back in the chair and watching the vague shadows of people slipping into the grounds and off into the beautiful landscape Victor had designed.

"Even with everything that's happened to me, I've never really been unhappy," Nichelle finally said. "Things have gone my way pretty much since I've been born. I'm good at what I do. My life is on track, and anything I want or need I've been able to get for myself." She tipped the pineapple juice to her lips and took a long drink, her throat moving as she swallowed. "Part of that is because Wolfe has always been with me. But it wasn't until he became the partner I never realized I needed that my life started to actually be something damn amazing."

She took a deep breath and turned to Mella. "Give yourself the chance to have true ecstasy instead of just the hot-chocolate-by-the-fire kind of life. Unless, of course, that's what you're content with." She balanced her nearly empty glass on her knee. "And if you are content with that, maybe you should leave Victor alone."

Mella heard the vague sound of other people coming into the room, nothing she hadn't been aware of while she and Nichelle were talking. But Nichelle glanced over her shoulder briefly, then stood up. "Excuse me a moment, would you?"

She rose, up and up on her ridiculously high heels, and made her way toward the bar just as her husband started moving toward her. They met each other halfway. Wolfe slipped an arm around his wife's waist and she leaned into him, brushing her cheek against his. Mella looked away. Watching them felt like an intrusion. She took a swallow of her drink and stretched out her legs.

The illumination from outside was soft and golden, the lamplight barely enough to push aside the darkness of the evening. Mella longed for some fresh air, and for Victor. The feeling was distracting. She took another sip of her drink and left the bar, and Nichelle and Wolfe's perfect love, behind.

Outside, the night was almost too warm. The humidity of the evening pressed against her cheeks, her bare arms, into the soft spaces of her throat. It was intimate and comfortable in a way that the house, even with its many chairs and softness and feeling of welcome, was not.

She held on to the railing and walked down the path toward the grounds, unconsciously smiling at the sight of the twin gazebos—one in the center of the maze and the other at the back of the property—that rose up like twin banners of welcome. She remembered arguing with Victor to have them built.

Her heels clicked against the flagstones on the moonlit path. When her shoes sank into the grass, she paused to take them off before continuing into the maze. The stone path turned to hard-packed dirt, and Mella followed it with no goal in sight.

Victor had done as she'd asked. The original manicured maze was allowed to flourish in beautiful chaos, its single path leading from the rear of the spice garden before branching off into multiple trails all the way to the end of the property. The tops of the seven-foot hedges had grown wild, twining together in a mix of greenery and flowers, a natural arbor.

From the plans he'd sketched for her, she knew there was more than one way to the center, but there were also many dead ends that led to solitary benches or unexpected pieces of stone art created by local children. All of it was woven with wildflowers, scented jasmine, lantanas, hibiscus bushes fully grown and springing thick blossoms whose colors she couldn't see in the dark.

Once inside the maze, she could see just how wild the flowers had grown. The air was thick with natural sweetness from the blooms, untamed hedges encouraged to grow even wilder, flowering honeysuckle scenting the air as it wound through other plants and up overhead to form a series of natural canopies. Blossoms and leaves brushed her bare arms as she walked. The stars peeked through the lacing of leaves and white flowers, weaving silver trails along the dark ground.

The dirt pressed up into her bare feet and it felt good, that small pain. It distracted her from other things. Wanting a future that was not for her. Lusting after a man who would only be a heavy boulder in her treetop life. Looking at Nichelle and her husband had loosened a yearning in her she hadn't been aware was there. Their love was beautiful to see. But it also left her eyes burning.

"What are you doing here?"

She jerked her gaze from the floral canopy above her to see Victor only a few feet away, standing near a wooden bench. The moonlight dipped over his face, emphasizing its cool symmetry, the hardness in his eyes. He was wearing his trademark black, of course, hands shoved in the pockets of his slacks. Mella slipped her hands behind her back, hooking her index fingers in the heels of her shoes.

"I'm walking," Mella said. "I think that's fairly obvious."

"I didn't think you'd be here this early," he said.

"Nala invited me. And I wanted to come." Mella knew without explanation what he was saying. He'd only planned on coming to the gathering for Kingsley's sister-in-law, then leaving before the press and everyone else arrived for the second party. It didn't take much to see the truth of it in Victor's face.

Mella bit her lip. "I'm sorry."

He came closer. "What are you sorry for exactly?"

Good question. It would be even better if she could come up with an answer. The panic that had made her run out of his house after one of the best orgasms of her life seemed far away now. After so many weeks, that terror had faded away, leaving only disappointment in herself for acting like such an idiot. After that, she had just been too embarrassed to face him.

He had been kind and generous and so damn sexy that she'd wanted to drop to her knees and pull him into her mouth, gratefully and with pleasure. She'd wanted to share with him just how amazing he made her feel. The problem became how to make it temporary, just about sex, even while parts of her ached to keep him in her life for as long as possible.

Mella chewed the inside of her lip. Nothing ever lasted. Why did she even want to press the issue?

"I'm sorry I'm a coward," she said at last.

Victor sighed. "What do you want, Michaela?"

Should she say it? Would it make a difference? Half the time he looked at her like she was some wild animal he'd found eating the flowers in his garden. The other half, well, *she* felt like the hapless meal.

"I want what anyone wants, Victor. I want to be happy. But this—" she gestured between them "—hurts."

"Being with me or being away from me?"

"Both."

A pained look just about destroyed his face. "Then what—" He stopped and took a deep breath. "What do you want me to do?"

"I don't know." Her words were a helpless cry in the semidarkness. "When this started, I just wanted to have fun, but I know that's not your thing."

"Why don't you let me figure out what's my thing before you make any decisions for me?"

"But you don't want me, not like this. You don't like taste testers. *You* said that the day we met." Despite that, though, she had allowed herself to fall into him, to fall *for* him.

Victor looked at her for a long moment. "That was before I knew you." He drew himself up to his full height and crossed his arms over his wide chest as if preparing for a battle. "Now it's obvious it's just a facade you wear to keep yourself safe."

Mella sputtered, a denial on her lips. But Victor wasn't finished.

"Whatever you are, though, I want you. Just as you are. Wild and generous. Beautiful and brighter than all the stars in the sky."

Mella pressed a hand to the sudden flutter in her belly. *Really?* She stared at Victor, and the sudden embarrassment tugging down his lips.

"Is that too much?" Then he answered the question for himself. "No, it's not. This is me being honest about what I want." Victor relaxed his shoulders and confronted her with his open face, the emotions he always hid from her. Fear. Doubt. Yearning. "This thing between us can work, Mella. Just allow it to be."

Mella shook her head. "It's not as simple as that." And she wanted to say more, but Victor was coming closer.

"I felt how you came around my fingers, Mella. I know you want this, too."

Then his hands were on her, cool and comforting. By now, she knew the familiar sensation of her senses leaving her, the way he crowded out all other considerations except how good it felt to touch him. This wasn't about the ephemeral things she had chosen for herself

out of self-defense. This was about an undeniable desire. Something she wanted and could perhaps allow
herself to have. No matter how long it lasted.

"Please," she said. "I—"

But his mouth swallowed whatever else she wanted
to say.

The shoes dropped from her hands and landed with
a thud in the dirt behind her. His shoulders were hot
under her arms, the nape of his neck a rough seduction
beneath her fingertips.

He pulled her closer, and the taste of his tongue was
like starlight and wine.

Chapter 9

Victor had not been thinking about Mella. Not about the way she smelled, and definitely not about the way she cried out his name when her body clenched in climax around his fingers. In fact, he hadn't been thinking about her so hard that he wasn't surprised when she appeared in front of him, strolling down the narrow path under the twining jasmine and honeysuckle, the moon lighting her way. In her white dress and bare feet, she looked like a gift from heaven.

Then it only seemed natural for there to be some conversation that would lead to her being in his arms. She had left him in his kitchen with a very hard problem. But that didn't bother him as much as the way she left, with no excuses and that frightened look in her eyes. The last thing he wanted to do was scare her.

Not fearless and wild Michaela Davis. Women had said that about him in the past, that he was a bit of a monster, emotionless and frightening. He didn't want her to see him as that. Not her.

The sight of her in the moonlight made him forget all the things he'd resolved. And so he did everything to get her into his arms again, to taste her sweet mouth and hear her passionate cries again.

Under the flowering vines, Mella made a soft noise and pressed closer to him. The prick of her fingernails digging into his chest like a cat dragged him back to the present, back to her hot mouth under his and the heavy pulse pounding between his legs. His body ached to bury itself inside hers. All of him throbbed to have her every possible way under the moonlight. But that was his own mindless lust talking.

Reluctantly, Victor pulled his mouth away. "Whatever you want to do, that's what we'll do." He panted the words into her throat and strove for control. But her fingers slid up the back of his neck, raked over his head and sent shivers of want rocking through him. Damn. It didn't take her long at all to figure out that pushed his buttons.

"I want you," she breathed. "This is what I want."

Victor didn't bother to clarify with her whether this was what she wanted right now or what she could see herself indulging in for years down the line. He'd never been one for casual sex and, after reconciling himself to the fact that she was as untamed as he was rigid and that being opposites wasn't the end of the world, he wanted to show her it was okay for them to be together. Like this and any other way she wanted.

But her mouth along his jaw wasn't allowing him to think clearly at all. Her teeth scraped against the faint stubble, her tongue licked over his Adam's apple until he was swallowing thickly, his body poised in anticipation of what she would do next.

She was a dream under the flowered arbor. Her natural woman's scent and arousal mixed with the jasmine and honeysuckle draped around them to pull him even closer. Then he was the one who ended up on his back on the grass, the green smell rising up around them from the pressure of their bodies. Mella's thighs spread wide over him, braced on either side of his hips. She sucked at the hollow of his throat, her fingers dragging his shirt from its anchor in his belted slacks.

If he were a better man, he would stop her. He would stop her wandering hands and tell her they had other places to do this, that they would wait until she was absolutely sure this was something she wanted. But she raked her fingernails down his belly, sending a jolt of desire straight down into his sex. Someone groaned. It might have been him.

Her mouth was sweltering seduction, a hot and sweet insistence, tongue sliding along his, her hands touching him in complete opposition to the nearly passive way she had been in his kitchen. Now, it seemed, she was taking her turn to touch and to learn what made him lose his mind. And she was a fast learner. It didn't take her long to unbutton his shirt, have it open over his bare chest while she nibbled along the twitching muscles of his pecs, licked his nipples and stomach. She hummed against his skin, her hands fumbling with his belt. It only made sense to touch her, too, stroking her back through the thin dress, slipping his hands up her thighs, then between them to find the damp crotch of her panties and moving them aside.

Damn.

She gasped when his fingers slid inside her, hips undulating, breath hot on his skin. He was barely aware of her pushing down his pants, only the feel of her hands on him, not hesitant, but firm and hungry, instantly yanking him toward the edge of fulfillment. But he didn't want this to end yet. Not when she was so wet and making such sweet noises. He lifted a hand to push her away, but her teeth closed around his nipple, her tongue stroking it.

Victor sputtered out a heartfelt curse.

His head fell back onto the grass, and all he could do was rut up into the tight clutch of her fist that was somehow wet and giving the perfect amount of friction.

Heat seared along Victor's spine, a scorching flush gathering between his legs that was a signal of things coming to an end much too fast. He quickly sat up and grabbed her hands, gasping and swallowing hard. The air rushed in and out of his open mouth, in sync with his racing heart and the pulse that was threatening to leap out of his throat.

"Stop!"

She looked up, her eyes wide and lust-dark. She licked her lips but did not move her hand from him. "What is it?" Her low whisper was breathless, a sign that she was eager to go back to what he'd stopped her from doing. But Victor knew if she kept touching him, it would be all over. He'd wanted her for so long, that one more touch and she would have the evidence of his excitement all over her hands.

"Michaela…" He moved his finger inside her, and she shivered over him. "Let me please you."

"You've already done that," she whispered against his mouth. "Now it's my turn." Mella licked her lips, and the promise in that one motion almost undid Victor. He twitched in her hand, hard and eager for a taste of her mouth.

But he pulled her up, kissing the protest from her lips, then pulled the jacket from his shoulders to spread it on the ground. Victor guided her to her knees on top of the jacket. "Let me take care of you."

He kissed the fragrant line of her neck, her shoulders. She smelled so good, like limes and the salt of her desire. His mouth pricked wet with the need to taste her.

Victor touched her, and she gasped. "What are you— Oh!"

Mella didn't realize she was on her knees until she was pressing into Victor's hand between her legs. Her eyes fluttered closed at the bolt of lust that shot through her. By the time she opened her eyes, the hand was stimulating her from a different direction, and Victor was no longer in front of her.

His breath brushed the back of her neck in a wave of moist heat. "Close your eyes."

Her lashes fluttered down to her cheeks as his fingers continued to touch her, drawing pleasure out with each deliciously thorough stroke past the edge of her panties. Mella bit her lip, whimpering as she pushed back into his touch that was almost but not quite enough. The sweetness built up, receded and built again. It was maddening, but she didn't want him to stop. He stopped.

She sobbed his name. Parted her thighs wider for him. Blindly thrust her hips back for more.

"Shh. It's okay. I'll take care of you."

Victor pushed up the hem of her dress, baring her hips and bottom to his gaze.

"You make me so damn weak." His breath stroked her hip as he spoke. "I want to throw everything away just to be inside you and hear you say my name." Mella shivered at the dark and heady sound of his voice, whiskey and bourbon and Caribbean rum drizzled in brown sugar.

"Victor—please!"

"Yes, baby. Just like that."

Mella wanted to open her eyes, but her lids were too heavy, the anticipation of his touch like a drug.

"Beautiful…"

She had only a moment's warning, his breath hot on her bottom, before he jerked aside the edge of her panties and kissed her swollen and dripping center. Breath exploded from her. She helplessly dug her fingers into the grass through his blazer. She widened her legs and sank back into the pleasure even as the elastic of her underwear dug into her skin.

The sound of his mouth rasping against the thatch

of pubic hair, the wet kiss of his lips on her lips, his tongue lapping up her arousal. It was almost too much. Mella shuddered and bit her lip to stop the moans that wanted to fly free.

Yet she knew she had to be quiet. She knew she couldn't cry out and moan like she wanted to. Even sequestered as they were from everyone else who ventured into the maze, there was no safety, no guarantee they wouldn't be discovered.

But still…but still…

All she could focus absolutely on was the feel of Victor's mouth on her, his miraculous tongue that filled and teased her, the hot sucking motion of his lips, his hands that caressed and stroked her thighs, kneaded and squeezed her bottom.

So good. Oh, so good.

She rocked into the ground with each press of his mouth. Then he did something, sucked and fluttered, and she couldn't stop the sob that clenched her throat. Her head dropped down, her breath panted, her body sprung tight. He hummed against her, and she lost her breath again. Lost every ounce of control she had as she exploded and shivered on her knees under the canopy of flowers and stars.

"You're so beautiful." She felt more than heard the words he pressed into her skin, her body carried along on a tide of pure bliss. But she did hear the familiar sound of a foil wrapper. Felt the glide of his fingers along the sensitive flesh of her thighs as he pulled her panties down.

"May I?"

She trembled, still in the aftermath of her orgasm. "God! Yes…"

Then she heard the sound of his zipper, the condom wrapper tearing. Mella closed her eyes tight, savoring the sensation of him tracing the blunt head of his sex in the river of her satisfaction. She caught her lip between her teeth as pleasure nipped at her once again.

"Yes…"

He pushed into her with a low groan. Then she froze at the sound of voices drifting close. But whoever it was had wandered onto the parallel path. She heard them through the wall between them. Mella froze. Did they hear her with Victor? Would they—

Then Victor moved, and she didn't care about them anymore.

He slid into her with a slow and delicious stroke that pushed a harsh breath from her throat. She tipped her hips up for him, urging him deeper. Victor bit her shoulder to smother his groan, his hips rolling into hers. The heat and size of him made her moan again, as quietly as she could, aware of where they were, the fear of getting caught ratcheting up her arousal until her belly was shuddering from each gasping breath. Victor moved with her as if he had nowhere he needed to be but inside her.

It was slow and hot, and she squeezed her eyes shut and focused on the feel of him inside her, the incredible fullness of him, the soft words he hissed into her skin, as though she was the most precious thing in the world, her body a place he would worship for as long as he drew breath. Victor was as relentless as the tide, unhurried but undeniable, his every breath slow and even. But Mella was impatient. She wanted to feel him lose control, wanted him to feel like she did, absolutely unmoored and unhinged from reason.

The slow fire had done its work, and she felt her house was about to burn all the way down. But Victor was moving behind and inside her still as if satisfaction was far away from him.

Mella quietly gasped his name, squeezed her internal muscles and reached frantically back to touch him. He grabbed her hand. Their fingers entwined. She felt the angle change, his body dip low. A sound rumbled from him, sinking into her skin. Then his breathing sped up. She squeezed again. He gasped, and dimly she heard the hesitation of voices nearby, speech pausing as someone asked, "What was that?"

But Victor didn't seem to care. Now he was the one past reason, and Mella felt a jolt of pride the moment before he rammed inside her fast, then faster, the slapping of their flesh a quick ovation to the control she felt him losing. His grip on her hand tightened for a moment, a squeeze, and then he released her, his fingers sliding between her legs.

Their racing breaths synced, and then she was gasping with him, tumbling with him as the promised heat resolved itself into an explosion, and he was jerking against her, mouth open in a silent shout against her shoulder. A powerful tremor seized her, belly quivering, sweat falling into her eyes, the scent of crushed grass and female desire and masculine satisfaction.

Then she couldn't hold herself up anymore. Her trembling hands gave out, but he caught her.

Victor whispered softly to her until they ended up together on their sides facing each other. She held on to him as she slowly floated back to earth.

"I'm sorry I walked out on you the other day," she whispered.

"I know."

His breath brushed against her mouth, and she was kissing the flavor of herself from his tongue. She dug her fingers into his bared chest, giving herself over to the wet movement of her mouth against his. Then he pulled abruptly away from her.

"Someone is coming."

She didn't question how he knew, just scrambled to her feet and yanked down her dress, quickly finding and stuffing her panties into her purse. By the time she had herself together, he was already zipped up, shirt buttoned and black blazer back on. But his eyes were still tender in the silver glow of the moon. She wanted to kiss him again. Mella deliberately stepped away from him when she heard the approaching footsteps for herself.

"I should go." She clasped her purse tightly against her thighs, turning her back to the path so she wouldn't see who was coming. Resentment at the intruders lay heavy and bitter at the back of her throat. "Call me tomorrow?"

"Of course." He dipped his head, the corner of his mouth curving up. "Answer your phone?"

She was thankful for the relative darkness as heat rushed into her cheeks. "I will."

He nodded again. Then she turned and walked away, aware of the sweet throbbing between her legs with each step.

The rest of the party was a blur to Mella. She knew it was a success, though. Everyone loved Sanctuary, from the full-size beds in every room to the biking trail winding through the entire property.

She talked with everyone involved in the efforts to make Sanctuary a reality, including Kingsley, who was absolutely unrepentant about "volunteering" Victor's services for the renovation. It was still early when exhaustion suddenly hit her, and her body told her it was time to go home. She was walking down the front steps of the porch, away from the bright lights and loud music, when Nala called out to her. Mella turned around, breathing deeply of the moist night air.

"I know I've been saying it all night, but I can't thank you enough for helping to make this possible." Nala came down the last three steps to clasp her hands. The crystals in her dress sparkled in the light. "You're amazing."

Mella fought back a yawn, but still warmed with pleasure from the compliment. "Anyone else would have done the same thing," she said.

"That's not true and you know it. You took this dream of mine and made it into a beautiful reality. The kids are moving in here tomorrow, and that's freakin' amazing." Nala drew Mella in for a hug, enveloping

Mella in her fresh tangerine scent. "If there's anything I can do for you, ever, please let me know."

"I never did this expecting to get compensation." Her voice was muffled in Nala's long hair.

Nala drew back. "I know. And that's part of what makes you so damn amazing."

"I'm happy it all came together." Mella glanced up at the house, the lights on, the joyous place that looked so different from the cold and worn-down place she'd seen a year before. "This place will blow the kids away." She bit her lip, thinking suddenly of her own home when she was a child, hardly a mansion but a place of love with her parents and their friends and things she could call her own without the fear of losing them.

"What?" Nala leveled a querying gaze at her.

Mella stroked her tongue over the question that lay just on the inside of her lips. She opened her mouth and let it out. "How do you allow people in your life when they can so easily be taken away?" Nala's brows rose in surprise, but Mella continued. "Aren't you scared that something will happen, anything, and take away Nichelle or anyone else you care about?"

Mella knew their situations weren't the same. Nala had only been a baby when her parents were killed. She'd never known them and had been brought up in boarding schools and by a team of family lawyers. She hadn't been old enough to miss the love she once had.

But the dawning look in Nala's eyes said she understood. She shrugged, the corners of her mouth turning down.

"I grab on to everything I can before life takes it all

away. Happiness can be gone in an instant, but that's okay." She stepped close to hold Mella in an unblinking gaze. "Don't put yourself in an emotional prison because of your past. It's not worth it." She smiled suddenly and gently slapped Mella's hip. "Now go and get that man."

Mella blushed. "Okay, fine." If her smile was a little bit shy, she could always blame the drinks she'd had that night. "I'll see you later on in the week."

"Cool." Nala winked at her.

She waited until the lights of the mansion swallowed Nala's dark-clad form before she made her way to her aunt's car parked in the stone driveway.

"Everything okay, honey?" her aunt asked as she got into the passenger side.

"No, not yet." She buckled her seat belt and offered a tentative smile. "But it will be."

Mella didn't allow the week to pass before taking Victor up on the invitation he'd left on her voice mail to go to his gym. It was a happy coincidence that the gym was near Mella's part of town. The gym had limited hours and was already closed to its regular customers by ten o'clock, but for some reason, the owner trusted Victor with the keys.

A glitch with one of the espresso machines at the Coconut Grove café kept Mella busy until almost eleven. Victor had been similarly delayed at work, more so by his own perfectionist tendencies than a temperamental machine that needed to be fixed before the morning rush, but the results were the same. Neither of them wanted to cancel their delayed eight o'clock date.

They met at the gym close to midnight.

Anticipation fluttered in Mella's stomach. She knew they weren't meeting to have sex. She knew there had been no agreements except to see where this thing between them could lead. That didn't stop her from imagining what Victor would taste like. Wondering if he would let her ride his sweat-slicked hips to their mutual satisfaction on the floor of the gym, or if he would flip her over on her back to take control. She packed condoms in her bag, just in case.

In the parking lot, she waited nervously in her car for Victor to get there. The lights of his boxy SUV swept over the darkened parking lot as he turned in. The car really did suit him, with its solid lines and predatory quiet.

He climbed out of the truck, already wearing sweatpants and a T-shirt in his usual black. Mella got so caught up in watching him walk toward her that she was still in her car when he leaned down to knock on her window.

She'd never had it this bad before. It was a little embarrassing.

Grab everything. That was what Nala said, right? She was willing to try it, especially after the conversation—and sex!—she and Victor had had the night of the party.

She got out of the car and grabbed her gym bag from the trunk, the butterflies still twisting in her belly. Should she kiss Victor hello? Hug him? He took the decision out of her hands by leaning in for a hug.

"I hope this place isn't making you uncomfortable," he said.

Glad for someplace to look besides his gorgeous

face and body, she cast her eyes over the small building with the old-fashioned lettering that said Darnel's
Gymnasium and Recreational Center. It could have
been straight out of a Gordon Parks photograph from
the 1950s. Minus the whites-only signs, of course. "Not
at all." She hitched her bag over her shoulder. "It has
character. I can't wait to see what's inside."

He gestured toward the narrow, one-story building,
his hand landing at the small of her back. "Shall we?"

It was hard not to shiver at his touch. This man
had her firmly under his spell. Everything about him
tore her composure to shreds. Mella walked ahead of
him into the building once he unlocked it with his
key. The gym was small, containing only a boxing
ring, a fighting cage for mixed martial arts, a space
for weight lifting that was thick with the smell of iron
and old sweat, and an open area with a half dozen wall-
mounted heavy bags.

"The bathrooms are over there if you need to change."

Mella pulled the rolls of red hand and foot wraps
out of her bag. "I'm ready."

She started to wrap up her hands. After a smiling
look at her, Victor began doing the same, spreading
his fingers wide to wrap the black cotton around them,
along with his knuckles and wrist. The process was
slow and mesmerizing, done in silence that was oddly
comfortable. After she finished wrapping her feet,
Mella drank some water from her bottle and started
her warm-up exercises.

He soon joined her in stretching, although she was
aware of him watching her form almost as much as he

was attending to his own body. But it would be hypocritical of her to say she wasn't watching him, too.

The minutes passed, and her body grew warmer with each stretch, her breaths deepening, muscles getting loose. All the while, she watched him, the big muscles of his arms and shoulders, the thick mound of his butt under the gray sweatpants. Mella blinked, swallowed and dipped her head briefly to pay attention to what she was doing. The next time they were together, and she closed her eyes to imagine this, she would sink her fingers into that firm butt and grip him while he—

"Are you ready?"

Victor stood only a few feet away, tall and gorgeous, bouncing lightly on his feet. She flushed, realizing she'd fallen deep into a fantasy and missed not only the last of his stretches, but him making his way across the room to her. Good thing her body was on autopilot and knew what it needed to do. Mella got to her feet.

"The real question is, are *you* ready?" Mella smiled at Victor and felt the laugh lines on her face deepen even more with his answering grin. He really was a gorgeous man. The serious side of him, the side that didn't laugh as much as other people, only meant that his face was smooth and unlined, a place for rare smiles to blossom and make the lucky recipient's heart beat a little faster. Like hers was now. But she'd happily blame that on her five-minute stretching routine.

"Practice with the bag and then spar?"

"Yeah. Let's go."

They approached neighboring heavy bags and immediately started in, throwing blows at the hanging leather bags, the sound of fists and feet connecting, their soles landing heavily on the floor. It wasn't long before they were both breathing hard, kicks landing firm and fast. Their breaths panted in the room, loud and rough. Mella fell into the rhythm of her jabs and kicks, aware of Victor, but not so much so that he was a distraction. He landed a hard blow and the ceiling-mounted bag shook hard, rattling the attached chains.

Mella stepped back, bouncing on the balls of her feet, her body warm and damp with sweat. "Time for a break?"

"Why not?" He dropped his fists and stretched his neck. "It's been a long week."

"Ready to take some of that out on me?"

"Not in the way I'd really like, but maybe later?" His eyebrow rose to tease, and she blushed despite all the things they'd already done together.

With her face still hot, she grabbed her water bottle and drank deeply from it. "Definitely later."

She cleared her throat, eager to change the subject to something a bit tamer. "You're a pretty good kick-boxer." And Victor was.

Mella expected Victor to excel at anything he put his mind to, whether it was cooking, kickboxing or bringing her to the very heights of pleasure. His body was a muscled, powerful thing, and he wielded it with a control that made her knees weak and her thighs shake with arousal. Maybe it hadn't been the best idea to challenge him to kickboxing. The sight of him covered in sweat alone was enough to test her self-control. But, really, they hadn't even gotten started.

"Thank you," he said. "*Your* skills are impressive." She didn't imagine the thorough visual sweep he gave her body. His mouth twitched with humor. "I'm not surprised."

"Good. Then you won't be surprised when I take you down and make you cry like a baby." She took one last sip of water and put away the bottle. It thumped heavily against the floor.

"You're a bloodthirsty little thing, aren't you?"

"No blood. I'm just looking forward to making you beg for mercy."

His eyebrows perked up. "You can try." His throat worked as he swallowed from his bottle, and a trickle of water dripped from his mouth down to his jaw.

Mella couldn't stop her tongue from flicking out to the corner of her mouth as if she could taste Victor's water on her own skin. She drew in a silent sigh. Why was this man driving her crazy?

"Prepare for your pride, and your giant body, to take the fall," she said, moving toward the larger grappling area.

The corners of his eyes crinkled as he seemed to fight a full-on smile. He put his water away and fell in step with her. "I feel we should make some sort of bet."

She tapped her chin, pretending to think about what she wanted. The truth was she'd been thinking about her next date with Victor for a while now. And she wanted a do-over of their dinner. And maybe this time, he would be the one spread out on the kitchen island and at her mercy. "How about you make me dinner once you lose? That should be simple enough."

This time, Victor did laugh, chuckling loud enough to make the sound echo. "I like a confident woman."

The laughter disappeared once they squared off. Mella hadn't worn any loose clothes on purpose. They'd agreed to kickboxing, but she didn't know what other martial arts he knew. She didn't want to give him anything to hold on to and put her at a disadvantage. Victor nodded once, then stepped back. "Ready."

She flew at him with a quick punch-kick combination, easy, just to check his technique. He effortlessly blocked her, slapping away her leg with a smug look. She jerked her chin up at him when all he came back with was a weak jab to her belly that she easily avoided, and a high spinning kick aimed at least a foot above her head.

Mella knew he was taking it easy on her, telegraphing his every move so she knew what was coming, but she was tired of him treating her like a kid. She tapped his back with her foot, a slapping kick that stung. Victor's eyes narrowed, and she grinned in triumph as he came quickly at her with a right cross she barely managed to avoid, dancing away from the swift breeze of his fist.

Okay. Finally.

And it was on.

The next hour was an intoxicating cocktail of kicks and panting breaths and punches and the slap of skin on skin that made Mella forget everything else. Her body felt vibrant and alive, capable of anything. The sweat ran down her back, over the waistband of her panties. She was aware of every aspect of her body, how Victor reacted and seemed to throw everything into either avoiding her blows or scoring delicate, stinging taps in retaliation for her carelessness.

She knew he was all in when he spun into a high kick, actually aiming for a hit this time.

Damn, he was sexy.

Mella dropped down to his unguarded belly, landed two shots and darted away again. Victor staggered back with a surprised laugh and came for her with his teeth flashing. Unimpressed, she swept his feet from under him with a low kick. His back thudded into the padded floor, leaving a man-size sweat stain on the mat. But before she could savor her victory, a hand wrapped around her knees and dragged her to the floor. Victor's body cushioned her fall before he abruptly switched positions, pinning her to the floor with his damp, heaving body, his breath panting hotly in her face.

He dropped his head, his wet forehead slotting into her throat.

"Gross!" She jerked away from his sweat-covered skin, or at least tried to. "You're dripping all over me!"

But he only pushed more into her, the salty scent of his sweat overwhelming her. "Did you wear these tight clothes on purpose?" He fit a hand around her hip encased in slim-fitting capri workout pants she'd worn to yoga the one time she tried it.

Mella laughed breathlessly and tried again to shove away from his sweaty face and bare arms. But he was immovable.

"I did, but not for the reason you think." She shifted, arching her face away from him. "They're just more comfortable."

"They feel like torture. At least to me." Victor groaned. The sound was pure theatrics, but it sent a bolt of heat straight to Mella's core. He gripped her hips to steady her, his wrapped hands firm through the thin layers of her pants and underwear. "Jesus...you need to stop wriggling around so much."

"I'm not..." But she was. Mella twisted, and suddenly Victor's hips were between her thighs. This time, his groan was pure reaction. Mella's breath caught, and she bit down on a sound of her own at the feel of him, hard and hot, against her hip.

"Victor..."

Her body was already sure of what she wanted. Her ankles locked behind his back and she moved against him, shuddering at the quick spurt of pleasure. He gripped her tighter, rolling his hips into hers, pressing his hard to her soft.

Oh yeah.

Mella slid her hands under his shirt and groaned at the feel of his stomach muscles, slick and hard, against her fingers. He lowered his mouth to hers, and she greedily kissed him back. She pressed up into him even more, meeting each downward push of his hips with an upward press of her own. Between her legs, she was slick and ready for him. Just one—

The phone rang.

"No...!" She cursed softly. It was her aunt's ring tone. Normally she'd just ignore it. A moment like this, Victor hard and pressed between her thighs, didn't happen very often. But her aunt had been uneasy all day, nervous about something. Something that could be important. Mella dropped her head back against the floor with a dull thud.

"I have to get that," she gasped.

"Do you?" He circled his hips against hers, a filthy motion that made her mouth dry and other places even wetter. Mella was tempted. Oh God, was she tempted, but…this was family.

After she found out what was going on with Aunt Jess, they could get back to this and take it to its logical conclusion. She was looking forward to having Victor in a bed for once. Or maybe on a gym mat for now.

"I do have to get this." She hoped he heard every ounce of regret in her voice. "I do."

He let her up without hesitation then, and she just made it to the phone on its fourth ring.

She cleared her throat and scrubbed a hand across her sweaty face, hoping her aunt wouldn't be able to hear in her voice just how close she'd been to having sex on a gym floor. "Hey, Aunt Jess. Is everything okay?" Mella turned her back on the temptation of Victor still on the mat, the crotch of his pants tented, his face unapologetic.

"Everything is more than okay, Michaela." Her aunt's voice sounded rough, as if she'd been crying, or shouting. "Shaun got out today."

"Today? The hearing went our way?" She smiled so big that it hurt.

"Yes." Aunt Jess laughed, breathless and happy. "I've been with him since he walked out of that place. I didn't want to jinx it by telling you before he actually got out. But it's real. He's here."

"Wow! That's…that's amazing." Her aunt had been praying and hoping for this day for so long, for four long years. "Okay. I… I can be there first thing tomorrow morning."

"That would be great. I know he's looking forward to seeing you." Aunt Jess's voice trailed away, and the sounds of a conversation reached Mella, a rhythm she was intimately familiar with from her childhood. Her aunt wanted Shaun to talk to Mella, but he was reluctant. Either shy, embarrassed or not wanting to be bothered, or all three. Mella had visited him while he was in prison, but she and Shaun never managed to remain as close as they once were.

"It's okay, Aunt Jess. Let him rest. I'll come over tomorrow before I head to work."

"Maybe you can take the day off and spend it with us." Again, another rumble from the background. Shaun making more objections. Understandable if he didn't want to be surrounded by people on his first full day outside the prison walls.

Before her aunt could say anything else, Mella spoke again. "Let's just play it by ear, okay? Whatever Shaun needs is what we'll do."

Her aunt's excited breaths chuffed at her through the phone. "Right, right. That makes sense. So, see you tomorrow?"

"Of course." She made sure her aunt heard the smile in her voice. "See you tomorrow."

Mella ended the call and dropped the phone back in her bag. "Finally…" She sighed, happiness bubbling up in her chest. Her aunt had her son back. Now they all could get on with their lives.

"Is everything okay?" Victor sat up. He looked down at his hands and winced at whatever he saw.

"More than okay." She bit her lip, tasting her aunt's happiness. "My cousin…" She paused, knowing that not everyone thought well of incarcerated felons getting out of jail. But dammit, this was her cousin, her aunt, her family. "My cousin Shaun just got out of jail today. That was my aunt on the phone."

"That's good news?"

"Yes." She nodded. "Absolutely yes."

Mella sat next to Victor on the floor, her legs folded under her. The sweat was drying on his skin, his breath long since evened out. She wanted to hug him in celebration of her family's great news. But she leaned back on her hands instead, contenting herself with simply looking at his beautiful body. She wondered if she could get him to take off his shirt.

"What was he in for?" Victor looked up from unwrapping his hands.

Mella hesitated again, this time for a little while longer. But she didn't believe in lies, even of omission. And though it was a shameful thing that her cousin did, she wasn't ashamed for herself or for her aunt to have survived it. "When he was a kid, he…he messed up and got behind the wheel while he was drunk."

With her chin held high, she told him the whole story. As she spoke, Victor's face changed. The warmth leaked from it, leaving it as cold as the day they met. Mella's stomach tightened.

The seconds ticked by after she finished talking. She clenched her jaw, refusing to fill the tense silence with empty, babbling words.

Finally, Victor spoke. "That's something to celebrate?" His voice was an icy blade.

Mella, immediately defensive, crossed her arms over her chest. "Of course. My aunt has her son back."

"But that man your cousin killed will never get back his life. He and his family won't get a second chance from anyone four years later."

"Believe me, I know. What Shaun did was unpardonable. Unforgivable. But I'm glad the system forgave him enough to allow him back into my aunt's life." She'd been wrestling with what her cousin had done the whole time he'd been in jail. Her feelings around the deadly accident and Shaun's jail time were hardly cut-and-dried. Mella had been furious with him for his stupidity. And, of course, she couldn't help but think about her parents and how she had lost them. But she wanted her aunt to have her son back, even though he'd done to someone else's family what had been done to her.

She was sure Victor didn't see any of that conflict on her face. He abruptly got to his feet. "I can't have this conversation with you right now," he said.

"What?" She stared up at his looming figure. His entire body was one tense line, and he looked ready to go another round with the heavy bag. Mella stood up and stepped toward him. "Are you okay?"

"You should leave now."

Mella stared at him still, wondering if he was joking. But his stone face said he was anything but.

"I don't understand this." His ticking jaw, the way he stepped back when she stepped forward, all of it scared her.

"There's nothing to understand. This thing with us—" He gestured between them. "It just won't work out. It was stupid to try."

Mella drew in a hissing breath. "Are you serious?"

She swallowed again and again the lump that wouldn't leave her throat. But when Victor only turned his back on her and said nothing, she felt it like a kick to the stomach.

Her pride eventually came to her rescue. She braced herself to get up, her sweaty palm sliding against the floor. She slipped, embarrassed heat climbing in her face. From the corner of her eye, she noticed Victor bending to help her, but she jerked away before he could touch her. A stricken look crossed his face, but she ignored it and ignored him.

"Mella—"

"No." She jerked away from his outstretched hand. "You're throwing me out. You don't get to act like the injured party."

With trembling hands, Mella grabbed her bag and jerked her things into it—her towel, water bottle, tennis shoes—not bothering to unwrap her hands or feet. Only once she was at the car, the heels of her feet throbbing from her short walk across the rock-strewn parking lot, did she really realize what had just happened.

Victor had thrown her out and never wanted to see her again.

Chapter 10

Mella started her car with shaking hands and pulled out of the parking lot. None of what just happened made sense. A difference in philosophy about her cousin's past was nothing to throw a potential relationship away over.

Relationship. Yes. That was what she'd wanted with him. She swallowed thickly, disgust at herself rising like bile in her throat. She'd been ready. She'd allowed herself to fall for Victor, had been a single breath from telling him, and then after one phone call, it was all gone.

She didn't know she was crying until she tasted wet salt.

Screw this!

She never cried. Never. Misery churned in her stomach as she drove.

You need to pull over. The voice came out of nowhere. It sounded like her mother, a husky voice warm with tenderness. It had been so long since she'd heard that voice inside her head—longer than she'd been an adult—that Mella didn't hesitate. She jerked the steering wheel and yanked the car over to the side of the thankfully empty road.

She had never wanted this. This pain, this crippling sense of loss. This was why she'd avoided men who were heavy and serious like her father, men who wanted more from her than her breezy personality and promise of uncomplicated pleasures. This—she pounded her fist against the steering wheel—was everything she'd tried to protect herself from. Now it was all happening to her in horrifying reality.

She loved him. He didn't want her. As quickly as she'd given herself permission to love him, he'd grabbed that feeling from her and smashed it at her feet.

Tears ran down her face, a hot and constant fall that made her eyes burn and sparked a throbbing headache just behind her forehead. She was officially a mess. A handful of tissues grabbed from the glove compartment and stuffed into her face didn't help her feel any better. She fumbled in her bag for her phone, fingers poised to call her aunt.

Then she stopped. Aunt Jess was busy. She was the last person Mella needed to call. Not with this. There was no room in her aunt's life for sadness now. This was, despite all the things Victor said, a time for her to celebrate, not deal with Mella and her disappointments. She bit her lip until she tasted blood, leaned back in the seat with the windows up and only the sound of her thick breathing in the small confines of the car.

"Hello? Michaela?"

She looked down at the phone in her hand, not realizing she'd actually made a call. She blinked to clear her blurred vision. Nala's face looked up at her from the surface of her phone.

"Hey," she croaked.

"You okay?"

"Relatively." Mella didn't have the energy to pretend she was fine. "I'm alive, but I feel like crap."

A pause. "Where are you?"

"Somewhere in my car." Mella sighed. "I'm sorry I sad-dialed you. Didn't mean to do that at all." She cleared her throat and wiped at her nose with the pile of wadded tissues.

"Don't be silly." The noise of activity came through the phone. "Wait, are you driving?"

"Not anymore. I pulled over." She looked outside the windows again, finally noticing a familiar sign. "I'm in Wynwood. On North Miami, near the, uh…" A familiar blue sign caught her eye. "Near the pet shop."

"Okay. Stay there. I'm on the way."

Mella instantly felt terrible. Or at least more than she did before. It was well after midnight during the week. What would it look like if she dragged Nala out of her bed to come rescue her like a cut-rate damsel in distress? She wiped her nose again. "No, really. I'm fine. I'm just going to sit here in my car for a few minutes and then go home. It's nothing serious."

"If it's nothing, don't stand me up, then. I'm getting

in my car now." Mella heard murmurings in the background, a muffled conversation as though Nala was covering up the phone's mouthpiece. "I'm not far," she said. "Maybe ten minutes."

Mella didn't have the strength to argue. She ended the call without looking and closed her eyes.

It wasn't long before a tap sounded on her window and Nala stood in the streetlight, watching her with worry creasing her brow. Her long hair was piled on top of her head in an elegant updo. Crystal pins shimmered in the dark mass, and a sleeveless jumpsuit emphasized the slight curves of her body. A spiked collar jutted dangerously from around her neck.

Nala mimed rolling down the window. Mella chuckled weakly despite the pain in her chest. She pressed the button to put the window down.

"You know," Mella said. "I don't think anyone has manual windows anymore."

Nala snorted. "And people call *me* sheltered and privileged." She glanced over her shoulder into the mostly empty lamp-lit street. "Let me in."

Mella unlocked the car with a touch of a button and Nala slid in next to her, bringing the scent of cigar smoke and red wine with her. She sighed. Mella had the bad feeling she'd just pulled the other woman from a very good party.

"You didn't have to come," she said quickly.

"I don't have to do anything but stay black and die." Nala rolled her head on the headrest to watch Mella. "I wanted to come and see you." She closed her eyes briefly, as if she was gathering her most serious self, pushing aside any remaining lethargy from her party. "So tell me, what has you driving around in your workout clothes at this time of night?"

At the mention of a workout, Mella winced. "Remember when you told me to grab everything before life took it away?"

"I vaguely remember that, yes."

"Well, I might have waited too late. It's gone."

Nala looked confused. "Wait. What?"

"I waited too long. Victor doesn't want me anymore." Even as she said it, she felt pathetic, like she shouldn't even be thinking such a thing, much less saying it out loud.

"That's impossible to believe. From what Kingsley says, he's crazy about you. Things can't have changed that much in just a few days."

"I told him my cousin just got out of the clink, and he changed his mind, just like that." She snapped her fingers, trying to make light of it so her heart would get the picture and recover right-dammit-now.

"That doesn't make sense. I've only had a glass of wine and a few puffs of a cigar, so I'm not that messed up. Tell me exactly what happened. Don't leave anything out. And say it slow."

Mella curled her hands in her lap. She didn't want to talk about any of this. All she had to do was get over it, get over Victor, go out with her friends a few times and he would be out of her system. Talking about it was too soon, too raw. But her mouth opened anyway, and the events of the evening, even the hot make-out session on the gym floor, came out. With the words came more tears, and then she was sobbing in Nala's arms as if her parents had died all over again.

"I feel like such an idiot," she wailed into the dark silk of Nala's fancy jumpsuit. "Why didn't Shaun get paroled four months ago? At least then I wouldn't have even known Victor, and this wouldn't be an issue."

Nala made soothing motions on Mella's back. "This would still have come up. Victor's dealing with some heavy stuff. I can't tell you what, that's his business, but I don't think you should give up on him yet. He likes you as much as you like him. You just have to get past this."

"I don't think this…whatever it is, is something we can get past." Mella hated the tremor in her voice. She sniffled and forced herself to get it together, levering back up into a sitting position to wipe her face with the already damp pile of tissues. "He hates me."

"None of these things are true. Just buck up, honey. Everything will sort itself out."

Mella made a face and shoved the tissues into an empty cup holder. "I doubt that very much. But thanks for saying that."

"I don't say things I don't mean." Nala glanced behind the car as if she was looking for something or someone. "I don't have much experience with love, but I do see how Victor looks at you. He's not going to throw that away because of your jailbird cousin."

This was too much. Mella just wanted to pull her sheets over her head and shut out the world until the torn feeling in her chest faded away to nothing. She pressed her palms to her forehead where the headache still raged. "I'm tired of feeling like this," she muttered. "This sucks."

"Don't be dramatic, honey. Just hang tight."

Mella frowned. "Hang tight for what?"

The flash of headlights washed over them, a car pulling behind Mella's little Fiat.

Nala breathed a sigh of relief. "Thank God…"

They heard the sound of a car door slamming, and footsteps approaching made Mella turn around to stare out the window.

"Going my way, ladies?" Kingsley leaned against the window of the car, a grin splitting his handsome face. He looked as though he was taking pointers from Victor's stylist in his head-to-toe black. His jeans looked as if they were just about painted on.

Nala reached across the driver's seat to tap Kingsley's muscled arm. "I'm passing the baton to you, Diallo. Don't mess it up."

"No worries on that front, little lady." He winked at Nala and opened the driver's side door. "Come on, let's get into an adult-sized car for this conversation."

Mella self-consciously wiped at the remains of tears on her face and stared at Nala and Kingsley, one after the other, wondering what was going on.

But Nala was already unbuckling Mella's seat belt. "Go ahead. I'll be here enjoying the stars through this cute little moon roof of yours."

Then Mella found herself in Kingsley's massive red Range Rover, seated in the front passenger seat with the windows down and the low sounds of Anthony Hamilton on the sound system. Kingsley's face was as kind and vibrant with humor as the day they'd met, a day that seemed so long ago now. The same day she'd met

Victor. Pain stuttered in her chest, and she squeezed her eyes tightly shut.

"Victor is not a bad person," Kingsley said.

She opened her eyes to look at him, but looked away again, unable to bear the kindness in his face, the pity. "I know that. I think everyone knows that but him."

"Yeah." He blinked slowly at her in surprise, as if discovering something in her he never thought he would. "He *is* a good man," Kingsley said. "He deserves good things."

Mella felt exhausted, wrung out by her emotions and the inexplicable tag team therapy session Nala and Kingsley were apparently running. "Why are you here, Kingsley?"

"I'm here for my friend. He doesn't always know what's in his best interest." Then he shrugged. "Besides, Nala called me. I can never say no to her."

Nala wasn't into men. Everyone who talked to her for at least two minutes knew that. But Mella looked again and saw that Kingsley wasn't saying he loved the other woman in a romantic way. He was a man who made and kept close friends. Nala happened to be one of them.

"What did she tell you?" Mella asked.

"Nothing. But Victor called me and sounded like hell. When Nala told me she was heading off to find you, I put two and two together. I'm a bit of an emotional mathematician."

Mella rolled her eyes, not in the mood to laugh with him. She turned back to face the window. The lamplight cast a sharp yellow glow over her little Fiat, the gray sidewalks, the brightly graffitied building walls. The street brightened from an occasionally passing car, but most of Miami slept. This was the time when most people were already in bed, unless they were up to something, or couldn't sleep.

"Victor's sister was killed by a drunk driver when she was sixteen." Kingsley broke the silence with the worst thing he could have possibly said.

Mella drew in a sharp breath and held it. *Shit.* She might as well have told Victor that his sister's killer was just released from prison.

"He's dealt with it, but not really," Kingsley said. "I don't know the particulars of your discussion tonight, but I'm guessing that has something to do with it."

"Did…did they ever catch the person who did it?"

"No. It was a hit and run. She died at the scene. The entire family is still messed up about it."

"Oh my God." Mella covered her mouth in horror.

There she was celebrating that her cousin had a chance at life again, while Victor's sister was six feet under because of someone like Shaun. No wonder he hadn't wanted to hear what she had to say.

"It's not your fault," Kingsley said. "Victor doesn't tell everyone about this. The day we met you would have been her thirtieth birthday. He's been really vulnerable for the past few months." Kingsley tapped his fingers on the steering wheel, a single and thoughtful tattoo. "Do you understand now?"

Mella took a deep and shuddering breath. "Yeah. Yeah, I do."

Victor left the gym and went straight home. He didn't know what to think, or even how he was feeling. The conversation with Mella—Christ, Mella!—had not gone the way he wanted, not by a long shot. The shock of her revelation was too much. It was only earlier that morning he was talking to Vivian and the rest of his family about donating to the city to install a memorial bench near where Violet died. And then this happened.

He felt like howling about the unfairness of it all. When Mella told him about her cousin, his fists had ached to slam into something. He'd been *this* close to breaking down in front of her. He knew it wasn't her fault that her cousin was a murderer and got to continue his life after a little four-year vacation. He was just someone else who'd killed and faced little real consequences because of it. He couldn't sit with her and hear any more about her poor, poor cousin.

Screw that.

He came in through the garage and into the house without turning on any lights, finding his way by memory and touch to the living room. There was already a light there, a single lamp by the high-backed armchair facing the bay. A familiar perfume scented the room.

"What are you doing here?" Victor went straight for the bar, opened the built-in minifridge and took out a can of sparkling water. The pop and fizz of the can exploded in the silence and swallowed his sigh.

He leaned against the bar and watched his sister peek over the top of the chair, her hair pulled back from her face, orange lipstick bright on her pinched lips.

"Kingsley called me."

"You made damn good time," he said with a twist of his lips.

"I was already up here." She turned until her legs draped over the arm of the chair. "I was planning on calling you tomorrow for lunch, but it looks like you may not be up to it."

"I'm all right."

"Are you?"

Victor's smile was more of a snarl. Without fail, she was always the one to worry about him. Not even their parents saw through him as cleanly as she did. Vivian was never fooled by his stone face. He took a sip of the water and hissed as the carbonation bubbled and burned going down.

"I'm a big boy," he said.

"Okay. Then use your big boy words and tell me what happened." She had a nearly full highball glass in her hand, an orange wedge perched on its edge.

Victor gave her the basics of what happened, skipping the part where he had every intention of making love to Mella on the floor of his old friend's gym. Maybe the revelation about her cousin had been for the best. Although he hadn't been thinking about it—or much of anything—at the time, there could have been cameras all over the place.

"Brother, one day you're going to make me hurt you."

"What?" He stopped with the water halfway to his mouth.

Vivian looked at him like he was nuts. "This is a woman with a big heart. The same heart you were crazy about just a few weeks ago. You can't praise Mella for her kind and generous spirit one minute, then turn around and punish her for it the next."

"What?" He felt like a broken record but couldn't seem to help himself. "Did you hear the part where I said her cousin got out of jail despite *killing* a person while he was driving drunk?"

"I have a perfect memory, and I was paying attention. Are *you* paying attention?" The ice clinked against the glass as she swirled it before taking a sip. "She didn't kill Violet. You didn't make a deal with the devil to give up happiness if he kept you from ending up like that asshole who killed her. Mella is an incredible woman. You've said so. Hell, even Papa likes her, and he never likes anybody." Her eyes were stretched wide in that look she had when she was trying particularly hard to convince him of something.

Victor bent his head, bracing himself against the bar with a tight fist. "I need to take a shower."

Vivian made a sound of exasperation. "Don't be an ass."

He put his half-finished water on the bar and turned his back on it. "I'm going upstairs. If you're still here when I get back, we'll talk about it more. If not, I'll see you tomorrow for lunch."

"Ass."

He heard the fondness in his sister's voice as he grabbed his gym bag and left the living room. His head throbbed with too many things. Her words. The look on Mella's face when he'd told her to leave the gym. The tangled wreck of the car Violet had been driving the night she was killed.

Victor clenched his teeth so hard his jaw ached. It was going to be a damn long night.

The next day, his sister stood him up. Instead of an invitation to lunch, she left him a note with his secretary.

Fix this. You're better than you think you are.
Prove me right.
—Your other sister

Kingsley was a bit more crass, but the message was the same. A message Victor received loud and clear when his best friend sent a strippergram to his house the day after Vivian stood him up. The girl in the knockoff Starbucks barista apron looked barely old enough to drive. She handed him a note from Kingsley, then sang, off key, the lyrics to John Legend's "I Can Change," including Snoop's rap. The girl was pretty to look at in her green apron and clear high heels, but Victor only felt annoyance at having to put up with her when he was far from in the mood.

He dismissed her with thanks and a big tip after she gave him a note from Kingsley.

Michaela is nothing like Patrice. If you can't see that, this little stripper is the only type of woman you'll get in your life. Doing it for money and barely legal. Get it together, Vic.

He crumpled the note and threw it in the recycling bin with the empty ginger beer bottles and the nasty note his sister left.

The crazy thing was, he wanted to fix this thing with Michaela. He just didn't know where to start.

Chapter 11

Fever was the only way Victor could stand it. Empty. He sat at the downstairs bar, music playing upstairs while the bartender Greg cleaned glasses as they waited. Victor's tumbler of ginger ale sat in front of him, nearly empty. It was his second one.

"Slow down there, man," Greg called out to him from the other end of the bar. "You're hittin' the sauce kinda heavy, aren't you?"

Victor restrained the urge to give the other man the finger, and instead calmly sipped from his glass, although he was far from calm on the inside. It was a Friday night, and the latest pop music thumped from the impressive speakers upstairs. Because of the effective insulation, he couldn't hear the stampede of people on the roof, the crowd dancing to the music, the muted sound of their conversations taking place above him. But he imagined it all. That's where she was. Victor glanced at his watch.

Maybe this was a lost cause. Maybe he shouldn't have bothered coming out. The ginger ale was flat and had too much ice in it. With its complete absence of other customers, the small lounge felt too quiet. He was hoping that would change soon. Hell, he'd been hoping that for over an hour now. Victor shoved his glass away and signaled the bartender for a fresh one.

"Let's just have a drink down here. Then we can go upstairs and dance. The bartender is cuter down here, anyway."

Victor heard the female voice floating down the spiral staircase, but he didn't turn to look. Beneath the thud of the bass, he could hear the clatter of high heels, more conversation, another woman's voice, soft and reluctant. Although the bar was empty, he sat where he always did, slightly in the shadows and out of the room's main line of sight. The high heels clicked across the floor and in his direction. He almost felt it in the air when the women noticed him, heard a swiftly drawn breath.

"I don't think—"

Victor slowly turned. The three women poised at the entrance of the room watched him. Only one was surprised; the other two nodded briefly at him and gave him what he easily interpreted as threatening stares before they gently pushed Mella toward the bar.

"Go have that drink, babe. We'll be right upstairs."

They didn't wait for her to respond. After another

look at Victor, Corinne and Liz disappeared back up the stairs, leaving a trail of sweet perfume in their wake. The door at the top of the stairs closed with a heavy bang.

Greg came over. "Hey, gorgeous. What can I get for you tonight?"

After a long look around the otherwise empty bar, Mella ordered something Victor didn't pay much attention to, only noticing that she didn't look at him. She stood silently at the bar, not even sitting down, and waited for Greg to make her drink. Her wait wasn't very long.

Once Mella had the drink in her hand, Greg finished cleaning the last glass and stepped from behind the bar.

"Good luck," he called out to Victor before heading out the same way Mella's friends had gone. The door banged shut again, but this time there was the sound of a lock turning. They were locked in the room together with no chance of anyone interrupting. Victor drew a breath.

"You know, I don't..." Mella swallowed loudly. "I can't do this." She grabbed whatever it was that Greg had poured her, something in a shot glass, and knocked it back. She gasped and made a face, then blew out a breath as if whatever she had deliberately taken into her body actually caused her pain. The comparison wasn't lost on him.

"You hurt me, Victor." She turned away from the bar, arms crossed beneath her breasts. "I don't know why you set this whole thing up, but you wasted your time. I won't. I can't do this with you again, no matter the reasons for you doing what you did. I'm sorry."

"Mella, please. Just listen." She had to understand he'd only been acting on impulse and out of pain. Victor stood. But he forgot how quickly Mella moved. She grabbed her purse off the bar and practically ran to the rear of the lounge, to a set of elevators he hadn't noticed before. She pressed a button and a bell instantly sounded, the elevator doors opened and she climbed in.

Then she was gone as if she'd never even been there.

Sanctuary was not even half-occupied, but it already seemed like a happy place, a place pulsing with life and new possibilities. Victor hadn't planned on stopping by, but on his way home from work, he took a detour to avoid a construction site and ended up at the open gates of the renovated mansion.

It only seemed natural to take the path up the drive and park in the nearly empty driveway. A dark green minivan was already there. It looked brand-new in the light from the setting sun.

Victor got out of his car and looked up at the massive four-story house with its lights on, beats from A$AP Rocky thudding from one of the upper open windows. A group of teenagers, four boys and two girls, sat on the porch, smoking and talking. They nodded to him in greeting, then went back to their conversation.

One of the boys left the group and jogged down the steps to greet Victor. "Hi! You're that guy we saw with Ms. Davis."

It took Victor a moment to place the boy, but when he did, he smiled and offered his hand, then his name.

"I'm DeAndre."

The boy was still thin, just like the last time Victor saw him at Café Michaela, but his face was less haunted, his clothes clean. "You here to make sure we're not tearing stuff up?" Although there was a joking lilt to his voice, the way he held his shoulders, slightly tense as if expecting Sanctuary to be taken away from him at any moment, made Victor tender with him.

"I'm sure you are all doing right by Nala and everyone else who put this place together," Victor said.

It had only been two weeks, but the place already looked like a home, filled with the vibrant energy of the kids who lived there. And that was only the impression he got from how the porch looked, how the kids ground out their cigarettes in an otherwise empty flowerpot instead of on the ground, the small pieces of furniture and artwork, bits of themselves, that they'd added to the grounds.

"The place looks great," Victor said. "Even better than before you all moved in. Are you doing well here?" He vaguely remembered that the kid had a boyfriend, that they were constantly getting into fights on the streets and in the youth home where they sometimes stayed.

"We're doing pretty good." DeAndre settled his bony behind on the last step of the porch. Victor sat next to him, politely refusing the cigarette the boy offered.

"Did you see Ms. Davis?" DeAndre asked. He lit a cigarette and blew the smoke away from Victor. "She was here, like, an hour ago. One of the girls asked her for some help filling out her McDonald's application. I think she was helping her with that."

Victor leaned back against a thick marble column and rolled up the sleeves of his dress shirt. "No, I didn't see her. Maybe she went home." But the words barely left his mouth before he heard the loud roar of a motorcycle engine. A familiar bike, turquoise and gleaming with chrome accents, rolled into the circular driveway.

"Here she is," DeAndre said.

There were two figures on the bike: a teenager clutching a narrow brown box to her belly, and the petite rider whom Victor easily identified as Mella despite her full face helmet, the leather jacket, jeans and combat boots.

It may have been his imagination, but Mella seemed to pause when she saw him, then waited a long time after the girl got off the back of the bike to turn off the engine and dismount. The girl took off her helmet and leather jacket. She looked barely sixteen and innocent, which was probably easy to misinterpret because of the piercings in her face and the tattoos down the entire length of one arm. Grinning up at Mella, she handed over the helmet and jacket, threw her arms around the smaller woman and, still holding her package tight against her chest, ran toward the house.

"Hey there," she greeted Victor as she ran past, a stampeding herd of one.

"Good evening," Victor said.

The girl giggled and looked over her shoulder at Mella, who was only just now carefully folding the leather jacket into the bike's saddlebag. "Your man is a hottie."

Mella ducked her head to fasten her helmet to the handlebars. Was she hiding a smile? A scowl? Then the girl ran up to the group sitting in a circle on the porch. "She got us a computer, guys!"

One of the girls who was smoking on the porch abruptly stubbed out her cigarette and stood up. "Word?"

After a flurried discussion Victor didn't even try to follow, the two girls dashed into the house, their feet slapping the marble as they ran.

"Hey, Ms. Davis." DeAndre stood up like a proper gentleman while Victor could only stare. It had been less than a week since that ill-advised ambush at Fever. A week plus since the night at the gym. Not a word exchanged in all that time. This was Victor's new definition of hell.

Mella greeted the boy with a light touch on his shoulder, smiling with her whole self. Until she turned to Victor. Then she stood with her hands in the pockets of her leather jacket, feet braced wide, her face blank. The lowering sun surrounded her like a halo. She was breathtaking.

Victor stood up. "It's good to see you."

"Is it?" She looked like a badass in her motorcycle gear, tough and unforgiving.

"Anyways." DeAndre cleared his throat. "I'll go…

uh…see what's up with Clara and the new computer."
Then he turned and left them alone.

The other kids on the porch sat watching Victor
and Mella as if they were part of their entertainment,
something they had unexpectedly found on TV. Victor
swallowed and tried not to look as nervous as he felt.
"Come for a walk with me?"

She looked like she wanted to say no, her eyes hard
and blank.

"Please."

Mella jingled the bike keys in her pocket, looking
past him to the snickering kids on the porch. "Okay,"
she murmured, the picture of reluctance.

Victor quietly released the breath he hadn't realized he was holding. They turned as one and walked
in the direction of the maze without exchanging another word. The sun was quickly disappearing. With
each step, night seemed to fall faster, leaving the evening shadowed and spiced with the fading sounds of
the kids in the house, their music, their laughter. As
they drew closer to the maze, the scent of the jasmine
grew stronger. Their footsteps faded into silence as
they left the stone walk and ventured to the grass and
the high, wild growth of flowers. Fate, it seemed, had
drawn them once again to this place.

They walked in silence, side by side, into the arbor.
It was a design that Victor had created on purpose, a
hidden entrance into a parallel path that led nowhere.
Someone had to be paying strict attention to find it and,
by the untrampled grass growing lush and untroubled,
few had so far.

He was hyperaware of the last time they'd been in the maze together. The humid heat of her against his mouth, the soft sounds she made as she came apart under him. But this wasn't the time. This evening was as far from that night as it could get and have happened in the same lifetime.

Mella slowed, falling slightly behind him before stopping completely.

"Why are we here, Victor?"

He walked the last few feet to the seat he left there, a natural wooden bench that blended with the arbor. Victor sat, making room for Mella to join him, but she remained standing.

He sighed and looked away from the hurt on her face, a mirror of the expression she'd worn the night he told her they were over. "This is not an excuse," he said. "But I hope it's a reason you can see to forgive me for." He took a breath, ready to tell the story he'd never shared with anyone. Kingsley only knew because he had been there through it all.

"When she was sixteen, my younger sister was killed in a drunk driving accident." He was surprised by the way the words rolled from him—painful, yes, but not the acute agony he'd expected. "They never found the driver. It was a stolen car with liquor spilled all over the driver and passenger seats. My family was never the same after that."

Mella came closer to the bench but still did not sit down. Quiet waves of sympathy radiated from her. Before she spoke, it was obvious she already knew the story. "I know," she said. "Kingsley told me."

"Figures. He always has a hard time keeping his mouth shut." Victor wasn't even angry. Kingsley probably figured he'd never tell Mella on his own. Which might have been true with any other woman. But not this one. He would have eventually told her about Violet, and the other reason he'd become the man who stood before her. He could give her the spiel about not ever being able to forgive someone who drove drunk and took another life. But… "I was drunk that night, too."

He heard the rush of Mella's breath. She quietly said his name and dropped into the bench next to him. "That night, I was out with some people I knew. We were all drinking and playing some stupid game when my father called. The call sobered me up right away but…" This was so hard for him to say; still he forced the words out. "I was driving drunk barely an hour before that, driving someplace I can't even remember now."

Mella's hand touched his, and he flinched from the sympathy in her face. He kept going. "Nothing happened when I was driving, but that was just dumb luck. I could have been the one who killed someone that night. When I saw my sister's body and my parents' faces, all I could think of was that I could have been that driver." He took a breath past the ache in his chest. "I stopped drinking for good that night."

"I'm so sorry, Victor."

He could barely manage a smile. "I'm not telling you so you'll feel sorry for me. It's not even an excuse for the way I acted the other night. There's no excuse for that. I felt like I broke your trust."

"I'll survive it."

He knew she was being dismissive on purpose. He must have really hurt her. Victor carefully lifted Mella's hands into his. "I don't want you to survive me, Mella. I want you to be happy with me. Will you let me try?"

Mella blinked at him. "I thought you didn't…" But nothing else came out of her mouth. She tried again. Silence.

"This is a lot to ask, I know. Your response may not even be the one I want to hear. But all I ask is for you to give me a chance. What I did was stupid. I have my own issues. It wasn't my place to take them out on you."

Her hands in his trembled like they were birds on the edge of flight. Victor stroked the delicate fingers but did not hold them, allowing her freedom to pull away if that was what she wanted. She balled her hands into fists but kept them where they were.

"I felt like a fool," she said. "That night, I thought things were finally coming together for us."

"I know. I was stupid." He knew he was at fault, had seen the tendrils of her trust and honest affection unfurling toward him, and all he'd done was crush them. His tongue and his emotions had run away from him and made *him* the fool that night.

"You frighten me," he said. The admission burst from him, bitter and honest. He pushed forward. "You're just so happy all the time. You have no idea what it's like to lose something that changes your life forever." Too late, he thought of her parents and what she'd told him that day she came to his house.

She flinched and pulled her hands away from him

like the touch burned. "It must be lonely in that place where you've isolated yourself." Mella stumbled to her feet.

"Stay." He tried to touch her hand but grazed the protective leather of her jacket instead. "I didn't say that to drive you away." He stood up.

"Then why did you? You know I lost my parents. You know their deaths messed me up. Just because I don't walk around radiating cynicism doesn't mean losing them didn't change me." She jammed her hands in the pockets of her jacket. "But I don't want to live in hatred and misery because of that. The driver who crossed four lanes of traffic and hit them is dead. I can't hate God. I can't hate the world. My parents' deaths are no excuse for me to live like I died with them."

Victor's ears rang with the reminder of the horror that had happened to her. And yet there was grace in her that allowed her to forgive the driver who had changed the course of her entire life. But that wasn't something he could dwell on just yet.

"Is that what you think I'm doing?" he asked. "Acting as if I'd died with my sister?"

"Yes. You've held on to this myth of never-ending suffering because it's easy. Although it tore me apart, I forgave that driver, I left my pain on that bloody road. I'm not saying I'm not affected in other ways, but I'm not going to hold on to my parents' loss as if it sucked any possible happiness out of my life. Yes, your sister died, but I doubt she wanted you to live like this, to never forgive, to build walls that only collapse to crush anyone who dares come into your life wanting more than a quick screw."

She stepped away from the bench. "If all you want is to give me an excuse for why you treated me like crap then, but want to keep pushing me away now, you can keep that. I'm not fine, but I will be." Mella straightened her shoulders and turned away.

He wasn't fine, either, and he wasn't sure that after this he would be. Victor took a chance again. "I want you in my life, Mella," he said. "Please don't walk away."

Beneath the hitch of his own breathing, Victor heard the light press of feet on the grass, someone coming to where they were. He cursed softly. Whoever the intruder was, they were on the parallel path in the maze, but that still meant the end of their privacy.

"We still have a lot to say to each other, Mella."

She crossed her arms over her chest. "Then talk."

He jerked his head toward the adjoining path in the maze. "Not here."

Mella frowned, then seemed to hear the other footsteps for the first time. "Okay. Come on," she said.

They went back the way they had come. At the driveway, he walked toward his car, assuming she would follow him, but a touch of her hand stopped him.

"You should come with me." She stood with her hands in the back pockets of her jeans, chin and chest thrust out in challenge. But the vulnerability was naked on her face.

Victor looked at the motorcycle, then back at her, this wild and reckless woman who'd come to mean so much to him in such a short time.

"I don't ride…pillion," he finally said.

A challenging smile touched her lips. "What? Don't you trust me?"

Well, that was the question, wasn't it? Mella hadn't broken any promises, only made him face up to the life he'd made for himself, and to the desire that had risen for her out of the ashes of his past.

"I do trust you," he said. "Maybe that's my problem. I trust you more than I have anyone in a long time. Trust isn't the problem."

She stepped close to him, all confrontation. "What is it, then? Is it love?" Mella defied all sense of personal boundaries and put her hands on his hips, leaning even closer. She smelled like sunlight and coffee. "Don't you love me enough?" She was trying to regain her sense of humor, was daring herself as much as she was daring him. But this was a game of chicken he could easily win.

"I do love you," he said. "Only *you* can say whether or not it is enough."

Mella froze, her fingers tightening on his waist and digging into his skin through the thin shirt. "You love me?"

"Of course." It was one of the few things he was certain about. "I thought you knew, and that was why you finally started opening up to me."

Her lashes fluttered madly as she stared up at him. She looked shocked. Pleased. "I… No. I didn't."

"But now you do." Victor watched as she bit her lip, trying to hide her smile.

"So…" The smile was all over her face now, luminous and wide. "My motorcycle. Your place. You make dinner, and we can talk some more."

He found an answering smile to give to her, laced his fingers together behind her back and tugged her flush against him. "That's the best idea I've heard all day."

"But the day isn't over." She looked up at him, all warmth and sunshine despite the shadows of evening around them.

"In that case—" he kissed the corner of her mouth, savoring the sweetness of her lip gloss "—I'm very much looking forward to the rest of it."

Mella pressed her cheek into his chest and sighed. "Me, too."

Epilogue

The card game was already set up when Mella walked
through the sitting room to find Victor. Three seats, an
unopened pack of cards. Three coasters for the drinks
that would come. She traced a fingertip over the back of
what would undoubtedly be Victor's chair. The action, as
innocuous as it was, sent a tingle through her. Even a year
later, she was ridiculously and completely under his spell.

Sometimes, she found herself wondering what it was
about him that had her so completely enthralled. Sure,
he was handsome, but she'd known her fair share of
good-looking men, and none of them ever affected her
the way Victor did. Maybe it was chemical. Maybe it
was because he was such a damn fine cook.

Speaking of which, the smell of food that had lured
her downstairs tugged her attention back toward the

kitchen. The smell hadn't been there an hour before when she'd left to take her shower and get dressed for the party. Mella followed the sweet and spicy scents to the kitchen.

The spice and the sweet led to Victor, crouched to peer through the glass door of the lower oven.

"Hey." She stood in the doorway of the kitchen watching his butt, round and firm, pressing against his faded jeans. He turned with a warm look for her, the corners of his eyes crinkling. "Smells good," she said, nodding toward whatever was on the stove.

"You look much more edible than anything I have cooking, though." He stood up, rising to his ever impressive six and a half feet, and discarded the pot holder, eyes roving over her with an appreciation that hadn't dimmed since they'd been together. She was only wearing tight jeans and a white, off-the-shoulder blouse, but he looked at her as if she were dripping in diamonds. Or spread out for him in lingerie.

Victor wore faded jeans and his favorite light blue shirt that was practically transparent from being washed and worn so much, the material stretching over his chest to give her more than a hint of his nipples through the pale cloth.

"You say the sweetest things," she managed a moment before he lowered his mouth to hers for a kiss. The natural electricity between them had tempered to become more of a constant current of attraction, something she had grown used to but still treasured. Their mouths moved together, sure and practiced, a kiss springing out of mutual love and adoration. Her breath hitched when his hands wandered low to caress her hips through her snug jeans.

Victor licked her mouth, sucked on her lower lip, and she felt herself melt in the most literal way a woman could when her lover caressed her mouth with the practiced ease of a connoisseur. Or a man in love.

"Don't start." She pulled back from him, breathless.

"I should be telling you that." He plucked at her hands that had pushed up his shirt and slipped over the ridged muscles of his stomach. It was an unconscious move on her part, and nothing she could follow through with. They didn't have time. But damn, he felt good.

"Tease." She tried to get her breath back, licked her own lips and could taste him, a hint of the coconut curry soup he was cooking, creamy and sweet.

"I can deliver if you want." He reached back with a practiced hand and turned off the stove, swept his T-shirt up and off before she could say anything else.

God. Damn.

Since they'd been together, Victor had grown even more comfortable with her, showing her a side of him that only his family and friends ever saw. Playful. Intent. Deeply loving. He stood in the middle of the well-lit kitchen, the light from the windows pouring over his chest, the starkly muscled pectorals, rippling abs, the teasing V of muscle that disappeared into the jeans sitting low on his hips. Her eyes dipped down. He was very ready to follow through with that promise.

She licked her lips again and took another step toward him, her high heels tapping on the tiled floors, hands already reaching out to touch his skin. He was so warm—actually hot from cooking in the kitchen for the past hour. He lowered his mouth to hers again.

"Oh, damn. Please put some clothes on."

Mella jumped and whirled around. At the sight of the woman in the doorway, she blushed and took a protective step back to shield Victor's arousal from the unexpected pair of eyes. It was his sister, dressed in head-to-toe purple, including a crown of flowers in her braided hair and velvet pumps on her tiny feet.

Victor made a noise behind Mella, a huff of annoyance. She felt him move, heard the whisper of cloth, like he was putting his shirt back on. "There's a doorbell for a reason, Vivian. And a phone."

His sister smirked at them. "And there's a bedroom for a reason."

"I don't know if you remember, but I live here. You don't."

Mella found herself blushing at the look on Vivian's face. She was clearly amused at nearly catching her brother having sex in his own kitchen.

Mella cleared her throat. "I think I'm going to... um..." She bit her lip, not sure what exactly she was going to do. She wasn't normally this shy around anybody. But there was something about Victor's brash and teasing family that reduced her to a stuttering teenager at times. Especially when they popped up when she least expected it.

"You don't have to go anywhere, baby." Victor clasped her hips to pull her back against him. "You know she's just teasing."

"I am," Vivian verified with a nod and an even cheekier grin. "But it's fun to see you blush." She came farther into the kitchen. "And it's fun to see my brother doing something spontaneous and enjoying himself."

"I would have been enjoying myself even more if you'd waited another fifteen minutes," Victor muttered.

"*Fifteen* minutes?" Mella turned to look over her shoulder at Victor, then laughed, meeting Vivian's gaze as she echoed the same words nearly at the same time.

"Christ. Maybe I'm the one who needs to go do something someplace else," Victor said, but he didn't go anywhere.

"At least it was me who walked in on you and not someone else. I've already seen what you're working with, and I'm not impressed." Vivian made a dismissive motion and went to the stove to take the cover off one of the pots and sniff what was inside. "You're making Thai?"

Victor ignored her last question. "You're the only one annoying enough to walk into my house without calling or knocking."

Mella reminded herself to have a talk with Vivian about that. As funny as it may be to Victor's sister, it made Mella wince to think of her walking in on her and Victor when they were really going at it. They'd had sex on the kitchen floor before. And on the counter. And on the window seat. Victor loved catching her off guard, and it made her heart race even more when he initiated something spontaneous, showing her he wanted her in new and different ways.

"I need to grab my purse." Mella touched Vivian's arm. "I'll be right back."

She wasn't very far when she heard Victor's low voice. "If you can't handle having a key to my house, I'm going to need it back." Mella giggled.

In Victor's bathroom, she freshened her lipstick and straightened her dress, making sure she was presentable before going back downstairs. In the mirror, she looked happy, cheeks glowing under the light makeup, her mouth still swollen from Victor's kisses, eyes glittering with happiness.

It had been an easy year. A year of changes as they both grew used to sharing their lives with each other. She spent most nights at his place and rented part of her house to her cousin Shaun, whom she'd given a job to at one of her cafés. She and Victor brought their families together for dinner once every three months and even already considered themselves engaged, although he hadn't officially given her the engagement ring he was "hiding" in the velvet box sitting in plain view on his dresser. It had been one of the happiest years of her life.

Mella smiled, and the woman in the mirror smirked, dark red lips curved like she had a secret. A juicy one. But it was no secret that Mella was happy and in love. She was also the safest she'd felt in a long time. She grabbed her purse and stuffed it with her keys, lipstick and phone.

Walking downstairs, she heard the doorbell ring and stepped into the hallway in time to hear the door click open, the overflowing of voices, greetings and flirtatious laughter. Corinne and Liz tumbled into the house with their signature raucous laughter while, behind them, Shaun came in at a more cautious pace. Vivian ushered them all inside with welcoming hugs.

"Hey, girls." Mella slipped into the mix. "Hey, Shaun."

"I swear every time I see your cousin he gets cuter,

Mella!" Corinne pranced through the hallway in a killer black dress and five-inch siren-red heels.

Liz shoved her way to Mella and kissed her on the cheek before following her nose to the kitchen. "I smell what that yummy man of yours is cooking!" she called out behind her. Mella shook her head.

"Shaun, you *are* looking pretty good," she told her cousin, who seemed to be doing his best to blend into the walls.

He had always been considered a "pretty boy" with his chiseled features and body that picked up muscle easily. Prison hadn't changed that. And, over a year after getting out, he was finally beginning to lose that high-alert look about him, as if he was on guard for threats and more than ready to meet them.

Despite his prison past, Corinne and Liz drooled over Shaun and often tried to lure him out to party with them. But he was more interested in playing cards with Victor and Kingsley on nights she went out with the girls. Otherwise, he kept himself at home most nights, watching British TV, and spent nearly all his free days volunteering with Mothers Against Drunk Driving.

"Thanks, Mickie." Her cousin bumped her with a friendly shoulder, his eyes warm and smiling. Before he'd gone to prison, he was someone who laughed all the time. But now, he had more in common with Victor with his guarded smiles and carefully given love. "I hear Victor's trying Thai on me tonight."

That had been one of Shaun's favorite foods when he was a teenager. "Thai with a dash of Southern flair," Mella said. "Kingsley wanted fresh baked biscuits."

Shaun nodded, another small smile making an appearance. "I think I can deal with that."

Vivian cleared her throat and not so subtly glanced at the bare skin of her wrist. "Time is flying, ladies. Happy hour waits for no woman."

"Okay, okay." Mella grabbed her cousin's hand, pausing when he flinched but didn't pull away. "Victor's this way." Shaun let himself be tugged toward the source of the smells, relaxing gradually under Mella's touch.

In the kitchen, Liz sat perched on a stool in front of a small bowl of soup.

"We're leaving now," Corinne announced as she brought up the rear. But that didn't stop her from grabbing a spoon of her own and dipping it into Liz's bowl. "Oh, this is good!"

"Everything he makes is good," Liz said. She'd given up her search for a man, according to her, in favor of eating everything Victor cooked. Because of it, she'd gained nearly ten pounds and never seemed happier.

Mella tapped Liz on the butt. "Let's go. One of Victor's dates is here—" she jerked her head toward Shaun "—and none of you girls are the second one, so let's go. We're taking Vivian's Jeep."

Laughter and goodbyes and quickly slurped soup, more looking at an imaginary watch and one open door later, all the women were flooding out the front door. Shaun stood at Victor's shoulder in the kitchen, sipping on a glass of ginger ale while he and Victor talked in low tones about something Mella couldn't hear.

Mella bit her lip, so happy she barely knew what to do with herself.

Against everyone's expectations, Shaun and Victor

had found mutual companionship in each other, Shaun looking up to Victor as a role model despite the fact that there was only a gap of eight years between them.

Mella cleared her throat. "I'm leaving, guys. Vivian and the girls will kill me if I make them miss happy hour." Both men turned, one tall and broad, the other slender and wounded, both looking at her with love.

"I'll see you both later on tonight, okay?"

Shaun saluted her with his drink.

"Early tomorrow is more like it," Victor teased. He pulled her into his arms to quickly taste her lips. "Be careful and come back to me in one piece."

"Yes, love." She inhaled the scents wrapped up in his shirt, of spices and sweat, and closed her eyes to savor him. Mella was dimly aware of Shaun turning away to rummage in the fridge, but she caught a flash of his smile. "As long as my body is able, I'll always come back to you," she said and slowly drew away from him, blushing at the ridiculously sappy but true sentiment that tumbled out of her mouth. To recover herself, she patted his solid chest, felt his heart thumping beneath her hand. "Keep the light on for me."

Victor chuckled. "Always."

Mella turned and waved at them behind her. "Don't get into too much trouble when I'm gone," she said. "Save it for when I get back."

Then she was out the door and down the steps, still smiling from the low and wonderful sound of Victor's laughter.

* * * * *

REQUEST YOUR FREE BOOKS!

2 FREE NOVELS
PLUS 2 FREE GIFTS!

KIMANI™
ROMANCE

Love's ultimate destination!

Turn your love of reading into rewards you'll love with
Harlequin My Rewards

MYR16R

"I understand whenever a Steele sees a woman he wants, he goes after her. It appears Tyson's targeted you, Hunter," Mo said as she leaned over. "Maybe he thinks there's unfinished business between the two of you."

It took less than a minute for Tyson to reach their table. He glanced around and smiled at everyone. "Evening, ladies." And then his gaze returned to hers and he said, "Hello, Hunter. It's been a while."

Hunter inhaled deeply, surprised that he had remembered her after all. But what really captured her attention were his features. He was still sinfully handsome, with skin the color of creamy chocolate and a mouth that was shaped too darn beautifully to belong to any man. And his voice was richer and a lot deeper than she'd remembered.

Before she could respond to what he'd said, Mo and Kat thanked him for the drinks as they stood. Hunter looked at them. "Where are you two going?" she asked.

"Kat and I thought we'd move closer to that big-screen television to catch the last part of the basketball game. I think my team is winning."

As soon as they grabbed their drinks off the table and walked away, Tyson didn't waste time claiming one of the vacated seats. Hunter glanced over and met his gaze while thinking that the only thing worse than being deserted was being deserted and left with a Steele.

She took a sip of her drink and then said, "I want to thank you for my drink, as well. That was nice of you."

"I'm a nice person."

The jury is still out on that, she thought. "I'm surprised you remember me, Tyson."

He chuckled, and the sound was so stimulating it seemed to graze her skin. "Trust me. I remember you. And do you know what I remember most of all?"

"No, what?"

He leaned over the table as if to make sure his next words were for her ears only. "The fact that we never slept together."

Don't miss
POSSESSED BY PASSION
by Brenda Jackson,
available March 2016 wherever
Harlequin® Kimani Romance™
books and ebooks are sold!

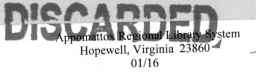